THE WEREWOLF
OF PONKERT

Author H. Warner Munn remembers that the idea for THE WEREWOLF OF PONKERT stemmed from a query of H. P. Lovecraft's asking why someone did not attempt a werewolf story as narrated by the werewolf himself.

THE WEREWOLF OF PONKERT

by H. WARNER MUNN

THE WEREWOLF OF PONKERT
by H. Warner Munn

"The Werewolf of Ponkert" - 1st published 1925.
"The Werewolf's Daughter" - 1st published 1928.

ISBN 978-1-64720-168-5

CONTENTS

INTRODUCTION

INTRODUCTION

    H. Warner Munn is one of those authors whose work dates back to the splendid, early history of Weird Tales magazine. "The Werewolf of Ponkert" first appeared in July 1925, when that magazine was slightly over two years old. Mr. Munn himself remembers that the story was inspired by a letter from H. P. Lovecraft which was published in Weird Tales. HPL asked -- and this was prior to the meeting and subsequent friendship of these two authors -- why someone had not attempted a werewolf story as narrated by the werewolf himself.

    "The Werewolf's Daughter" appeared as a serial in the same magazine in 1928, and Munn went on to write other stories in the same series.

Noticeably coupled with the werewolf theme is a
strong strain of gothic influence from the "last
and best of the gothics." The character of the
"master" has been compared with that of the famous creation of Charles Robert Maturin, MEL-
MOTH THE WANDERER (1820).

A New England native, Harold Warner Munn
was born in Athol, Massachusetts, and spent a
good portion of his life in the Athol-Orange region
of Massachusetts, which was also the home of the
late W. Paul Cook. Mr. Munn was visited, on
occasion, by H. P. Lovecraft, and was in contact
with many of the early Weird Tales group. For the
past twenty-five years he has been living on the
west coast in the State of Washington, where he
writes from an attic above his home. His published
books include THE WEREWOLF OF PONKERT
(1958), KING OF THE WORLD'S EDGE (1966),
THE SHIP FROM ATLANTIS (1967), a 1974-nomi-
nee for the best fantasy novel -- MERLIN'S RING,
and THE BANNER OF JOAN (1975), a series of
poems with prose interjections making up the epic
adventure of Joan of Arc. His short stories have
been included in BY DAYLIGHT ONLY, MORE
MACABRE, in Unknown, Weird Tales, Whispers,
Weirdbook, and Moonbroth magazines, as well as
in numerous amateur poetry journals.

Munn's avocational interests are witchcraft
and demonology, curiosa and trivia of all kinds,
poetry and art. He declares: "I like to take an
obscure fact as a foundation and base upon it fan-
tastic situations and plots." He adds that "I was
born the year the Wright Brothers flew their first
plane and hope to live to see Halley's Comet for
the second time and -- if I do -- may well hang
around long enough to also see a man set foot upon

the red soil of Mars. Will try to wait for these two magnificent events.

"In the meantime, I enjoy good food, travel, the society and the companionship of interesting people and lovely ladies and shall make a sincere effort to continue doing so until the time comes when I shall write -- and read -- no more."

THE WEREWOLF
OF PONKERT

PROLOGUE

In the past when I toured in France, invariably I made a point of never failing to stop at a certain tavern, about thirty miles from Paris. I will not give you more definite directions for reaching it, for it was a discovery of my own, and as such I would share it with no one. The fact that the inn has very pretty serving maids is but incidental, the real reason of my visits being the superlative excellence of the wine.

Many a night have the old Pierre and I sat, smoked and drunk till the wee hours of the morning, and many have been the experiences we have exchanged of wild, eery adventure in various parts of the globe. Pierre also was a great traveler and seeker after adventure before he drifted into the backwater of this placid village, to finish there the remainder of his days.

One night (or morning, I should say), Pierre grew indiscreet under the influence of his nectar, and let fall a few

19

words so pregnant of possibilities that I scented a mystery at once; and when he was sober I demanded an explanation. And, having said so much, seeing that he could not dissuade me, he brought forth proof of his dark hints in regard to a horrible occurrence in the annals of his family.

The proof was a book, bound in hand-tooled leather, and, locked by a silver clasp. When open it proved to be written in a crabbed hand in old Latin on what was apparently parchment, now yellow with age, but must, when new, have been remarkably white.

It comprised only four leaves, each a foot square, and glued or cemented to a thin wooden backing. They were written on only one side and completely covered with this close, crabbed Latin.

On the back of the book were two iron staples, and hanging from each, several links of heavy, rusted chain. Evidently, like most valuable books which were available to the public in the past, it had been chained fast to something immovable to prevent theft.

Unfortunately, I cannot read Latin, or in fact any languages but French and English, although I speak several. As a consequence, it was necessary for my friend to read it to me.

After I had recovered from the numbness which the curious narrative had thrown over me, I begged him to read it again—slowly. As he read, I copied; and here is the tale for you to judge and believe as you see fit. Told in Hungarian, transcribed in Latin, translated into modern French and from that into English, it is probably both garbled and improved. No doubt anachronisms abound, but be that as it may, it remains without dispute the only authentic document known of a werewolf's experiences, dictated by himself.

CHAPTER I

Having but a few hours in which to live, I dictate that which follows, hoping that someone thereby may be warned by my example and profit by it. The priest has told me to tell my story to him and he will write it down. Later it will be written down again, but I do not care to think of that now.

My name is Wladislaw Brenryk. For twenty years I lived in the village where I was born, a small place in the north-eastern part of Hungary. My parents were poor and I had to work hard—harder, in fact, than I liked, for I was born of a languid disposition. So I used my wits to save my hands, and I was clever, if I do say it myself. I was born for trading and bargaining, and none of the boys I grew to manhood with could beat me in a trade.

Time went on, and before I had reached manhood my father died in a pestilence. Although my mother was pestilence salted (for she had the plague when she was a little girl and recovered), she soon gave up, grew weaker and weaker, finally joining my father in the skies. The priest of our village said that it was the trouble in her lungs that killed her.

Alone and lorn for the first time in my life, I could not bear to remain longer amongst the scenes of my boyhood. So on a fine spring morning I set forth carrying on my back those possessions which I could not bring myself to part with, and around my waist a well-stuffed money belt, filled with the results of my trading and the sale of our cottage.

For several years I wandered here and there, for a time horse trading, then again a peddler of jewelry and small articles. Finally I came to Ponkert, and started a small shop in which I sold beautiful silks, jewels and sword hilts. It was the sword hilts that sold the best. They were highly decorated with golden filligree, and encrusted with precious stones. Chiefs and moneyed nobles would come or send messengers for many miles to obtain them. I gained a reputation for honesty and fair dealings, likewise a less enviable notoriety for being a miser. It is true that I was careful and cautious, but I defy anyone to prove that I was parsimonious.

I had closed up the shop for the night and harnessed the horses for the long drive home, when for the first time I wished that I lived in the village instead of being so far away. I had always enjoyed the ride before; a man can think much in a ten mile ride, and it gave an opportunity to clean my mind of the day's worries and bickering, so as to come to my dear wife and little daughter with thoughts only of them.

What made me look forward with anxiety to the long ride home was the many broad gold pieces secreted in my wallet. I had never been molested on that road, but others had been found robbed and partly devoured, with tracks of both men and beast about them in the snow. Obviously, thought I at the time, thieves had beaten them down, leaving them for the wolves.

But there was a disturbing factor in the problem; not only were the bodies horribly mutilated and the beast tracks about them extraordinarily large for wolf tracks, but the feet of the men were unprotected by any covering whatever! Barefooted men roaming through the forests, in the snow, on the slim likelihood of discovering prey which could be forced to yield wealth! The very idea was improbable. If I had only known then what I know now, my entire life might have been changed; but it was not so to be.

To return to my story: It was known that I had a large amount of money in my possession, for that afternoon the chief of a large Tartar caravan which was passing through had stopped at my shop and taken six of my best sword hilts, leaving their equivalent in gold. So I had cause enough to worry. I looked about for some sort of weapon, and found a short iron bar which I tucked beneath the robes of the sleigh; then I spoke to the mares, and we were off on the long ride home.

For a long time we went creaking along, the sleigh runners squeaking on the well-packed snow. Frost was in the air, and the stars gleamed down coldly upon the dark forest, hardly lighting the road. As yet the moon had not risen.

I turned from the main traveled highway and took the river road. This left the forest behind, but the traveling was much worse. Exposed to the winds, the light snowfall of the morning had drifted, and the roadway was choked. I thought of leaving the road and taking to the smooth surface of the river which gleamed brightly to the left, but this would have meant a mile or more extra to travel, for the river curved in a great bend opposite our home, and there was an impassable barrier of small trees and brush for some distance.

The moon was rising over the hill I had just quitted, and as the beams struck upon me, I was suddenly seized by a fit of the most unaccountable terror. This peculiar feeling held me rigid in my seat. It seemed as if a hand of ice had been suddenly laid upon the back of my neck.

The mares, it was evident, had felt this strange thrill,

also, for they had imperceptibly increased their speed without urging of mine. Indeed, I could not have moved a muscle while that spell was upon me.

Soon we dipped down into the hollow at the hill's foot, and the power that had frozen me was removed. A strange feeling of exaltation and happiness swept over me, as if I had escaped from some terrible and unthinkable danger.

"Hai!" I shouted, rising in the sleigh and cracking my whip.

The mares responded nobly, and we started to climb the next hill. As we did so, a fiendish howling came down the wind, but faintly, as if it were some distance away. I stopped the mares and stood up in the sleigh, the better to listen.

Faintly and far away sounded the cries, mellowed by distance. Then they grew louder and louder as the brutes came nearer, and over the top of the hill I had just quitted swept the devilish pack! They were on my trail, and it was only too plain that before I could reach home they would be upon me.

There was only one chance, and I took it. I clucked to the horses and turned them on to the ice of the river where lay a straight, smooth roadway. As long as the mares kept their feet, I was safe. But if one should stumble—!

Then that same spell of horror threw its icy mantle over me again; I sagged back; the mares took the bit in their teeth, and we rushed like a thunderbolt down the river.

Little puffs of diamond dust shot from the ice into my lap as the steel-shod hoofs rang and clicked. On we tore, while I sat in the sleigh like a stone, unable to move a muscle. Faster and faster we rushed between the banks of brush that fringed the icy causeway.

Fainter re-echoed the demoniac ululations behind me, until at last they ceased altogether and the horses gradually slackened their furious pace.

Here the spell left me, nor did it ever come again. Now we traveled at a trot, which slowed until the mares were but walking along, their panting breath paling their dark heaving sides to gray, in the frosty air.

Then we rounded the bend, and I saw black, open water ahead. Here progress, perforce, ceased. There was no way out, except to turn back and mount the bank where less underbrush grew, then into the smooth plain beyond and homeward.

So I tugged at the rein, and we swerved half way around. In that moment of unpreparedness, all became confusion.

A gloating chuckle sounded evilly from the farther bank, and five great gray shapes charged at me across the ice.

To think was to act with me. I have always been a creature of impulse, and almost instinctively I turned back, slashing the mares till they reared and we plunged straight forward into the onrushing mass of bodies. This resolute move took the beasts by surprise and halted them. They scattered, and I was through, with a clear road before me. But my escape was not so to be accomplished.

Silently, from the shelter of an overhanging rock, trotted two more of the creatures; a very giant of a beast, gaunt and gray, beside which moved a small black one. Roaring, the gray flung himself at the horses, which reared and plunged in terror; and the rest were upon me from the rear.

Then, turmoil of battle, pandemonium of sound, through which cut like a knife the scream of a horse. One was down! I felt the sleigh lurch to one side; heavy bodies struck at me, sharp teeth tore; but I kept my balance until one, such was his velocity, struck me and laid me flat in the bottom of the sleigh, himself rebounding and shooting over the side.

Something offered itself to my hand, something cold and metallic. I raised my arm, smote, felt steel bite bone, felt bone crunch beneath my stroke. I laid about me like a madman, with the bar, and cleared a space. I stood erect and waited for the attack.

But no instant attack followed. The menace of the bar was apparently too strong, and one by one they sank down on their haunches to rest or to wait. Jaws gaped wide, and tongues lolled. Panting, they rested after the long run.

As I stood there in the sleigh, watching them, it seemed as if they were laughing, ghoul-like, at my horrible plight. As I soon found, they were!

I became conscious of a noise behind me, a small noise such as the wind might make blowing a dead leaf across the bare ice; a sound like dead twigs rustling in the breeze, a faint scraping of claws, a padding of feet; and turning, I looked straight into the red glaring dots which were the eyes of the black wolf!

I shouted hoarsely, swung up the bar and brought it down with every ounce of force that I possessed. Unfortunately for myself, the beast, and Hungary, the great gray creature which ran at his side swerved and took the blow instead, catching him squarely between the eyes.

He grunted, choked; a stream of blood shot from his mouth and nostrils, and his eyelids opened and closed convulsively. Then he collapsed. The bar had crashed through his head.

I whirled, expecting to be overwhelmed by the six that still lived, but to my intense surprise the surge of bodies that I had seen from the tail of my eye, when I struck at the black wolf, had subsided, and they were now loping round and round the sleigh.

As they moved, the stricken mare followed them with her pain-filled eyes, while the one that was unharmed struggled constantly to be free. As the black leader passed me in the circling route, I, likewise, slowly turned to keep him always in sight. Instinct told me that from him would come my greatest danger.

Now I noticed a strange thing. About the necks of each of the five gray beasts there hung upon a thong a leathern pouch about the size of a large fist. These pouches hung flat and flaccid as if they were empty. The black, examine as closely as I might, wore none.

Then, as with one accord, they stopped in their tracks, and sank on their haunches. That for which they had been waiting had at last occurred. There seemed to be some sort of a silent signal given. Simultaneously they lifted their heads and loosed a long, low wail, in which seemed to hang all the desolation and loneliness of eternity. Thereafter none moved or uttered a sound.

Everything was deathly still. Even the wind, which had been sporting in the undergrowth, had now faded into nothingness and died. Only the labored breathing of the two mares and the hoarse panting of the brutes was to be heard.

Little red eyes, swinish and glittering like hell-sparks, shone malevolently at me by the reflected light of the now fully risen moon.

In this unaccountable pause, I had time to see the full beauty of the trap. As I have stated, the river formed a great bow, and while I was traveling on the curve between nock and nock, they quitted the river and waited at the rapids, the line of their pursuit forming the string to the bow.

Also, for the first time, I could examine carefully and note what manner of beasts these were that held me in their power.

Far from being wolves, as my first thought had been, they were great gray animals, the size of a large hound, excepting the leader, who was black and more the size and shape of a true wolf. All, however, had the same general characteristics. A high, intelligent brow, beneath which gleamed little red pig-like eyes, with a glint of a devil in their glance; long and misshapen hind quarters, which lent them a rabbit lope when they ran; and most terrifying of all, they were almost hairless and possessed not the slightest rudiment of a tail!

29

The circle was so arranged that as I stood, wary of possible attack, I could see four of the six. The small black creature was directly in front of me, tongue hanging out, apparently chuckling to himself in anticipation of some ghastly joke to follow.

Two were behind me, in whichever way I turned, but the night was so still that I could have heard them approaching long before they could have rushed me.

As I watched the creatures, I suddenly noticed that they were no longer glaring at me, but at something behind and beyond me and on the ground. I whirled, fearing a charge, but not a move anywhere in the circle had taken place. So I glanced with the tail of my eye for a rush at my back, and set myself to solve the mystery.

There was nothing before me, on the bare ice, but here and there a white line extended across the river, caused by the snow drifting into cracks. Now I noticed that across one of these there lay, inside the circle, the dead body of the thing that I had slain with the bar. The four creatures which I could not see were watching this intently. I did likewise, with senses alert for treachery. I glanced from one end of the warped, twisted and broken thing, to the other. Somehow it seemed more symmetrical than before; longer in a way, and of a more human cast of feature.

Then—God! Shall I never forget that moment?

I looked at its right forepaw, or where its right forepaw should have been and was not. A white, hairless hand had taken its place!

I screamed hoarsely and horribly, grasped my bar firmly, and leaped from the sleigh into the pack which, risen, was waiting to receive me.

Everything from that moment until my arrival home in the morning is a blur. I remember a black figure standing erect before me, burning eyes which fixed me like a statue of stone, a command to strip, and a sharp stinging pain in the hollow of my elbow where the great vein lies.

Then more dimly, I seem to recall a moment of intense

30

anguish as if all my bones were being dislocated and reset, a yelping, howling chorus of welcome, a swift rushing over ice on all fours, and a shrill, sharp screaming, such as only a horse in mortal fear can give.

Then there is a clear spot of recollection in which I was devouring the flesh and blood of my own mare, with snarling creatures like myself gorging all around me.

How I reached home, I have not the slightest idea, but the next thing I remember is a warm room and my dear wife's face bending over mine. All after that, for nearly a week, was delirium, in which I raved incessantly, so they told me, of wolves which were not wolves, and a black fiend with eyes like embers.

CHAPTER II

When I was well again, I went to the scene of my adventure, but the ice had broken up in an early thaw, and only the swollen river rolled where I had been captured. At first, I thought that my half remembered fancies were freakish memories, born of delirium, but one night in the early spring, as I lay in bed, only half asleep, something occurred which robbed me of this hope. I heard the long, melancholy wail of a wolf! Calling and appealing, it drew me to the window in hopes of seeing the midnight marauder, but nothing was visible as far as I could see, so I turned to go back to bed again. As I moved away from the window it came again, insistently calling. A powerful attraction drew me. I silently opened the window and melted into the darkness outside.

It was a warm spring evening as I padded silently along on bare feet, through the forest, drawn in a direction that led toward the thickest portion of the wood. I must have gone at least for half a mile under the influence of a strange exhilaration that had come over me, like that of a lover who keeps a tryst with his beloved.

Then the wailing cry echoed again, but with a shock I realized that there was no sound in the wood save the usual night noises. I realized the truth! The sound did not exist in reality, but I was hearing with the ears of the spirit rather than my fleshly ones. I suspected danger, but it was too late to turn back.

A figure rose to a standing posture, and I recognized the master, as he called himself, and we also, later. Under a power not my own, I stripped off my night garments, concealed them in a hollow tree which the master showed me, and fell to the ground, a beast! The master had drunk my blood, and the old story that I had never quite believed, to the effect that if a wampyr drinks one's blood, he or she has a power over that person that nothing can break, and eventually he also will be a wampyr, was coming true.

We raced off into the night, and when joined by the other five, paused for a time in the forest. Here the master transformed himself, and I also. We stood there, and for the first time I heard the master's voice.

"Look well!" it croaked. "Look well! Welcome you to the pack this man?" (From the tone and actions I judged that he was speaking by rote, and using set phrases for the occasion.) Here there arose a howl of assent.

"Look well!" he said to me. "Look well! Do you wish to be one of these?" pointing to the pack. I covered my eyes with my hands and shrank back. "Think well," he spoke again, catching my bare shoulder with one talon, and mouthing into my ear. "Will you join my band of free companions, or furnish them with a meal tonight?" I could imagine that a death's head grin overspread his features at this, though my eyes were still blinded.

"You have a choice," he said. "We do not harm the poor, only the rich, although now and then we take a cow or horse from them, for that is our due. But the rich we slay, and their jewels and fine gold are ours. I take none myself; all belongs to my companions. What do you say?"

I cried "No!" as loudly as I could, and stared defiantly

into his face. Over his shoulder I noted that the pack was gradually moving in, stealthily with eager leering looks.

"Ha!" he cackled, as I paled before that menace; "where now is your bravery? Make your choice. Die here and now, or make a promise to obey me unswervingly, to deviate not a jot from my orders, no matter what they may be, and be my willing slave. I will make you rich beyond your wildest dreams, your people shall wear sables and ermine, and the king himself will be proud to acknowledge you as friend. Come, what say you?" he asked.

I hesitated, temporizing. "Why do you single out me? I have never harmed you, do not even know you. There must be hundreds stronger than I and more willing, within easy reach. Why not use those you have or take someone else?"

"There must be seven in the pack," he answered simply. "You slew one, therefore must you take his place. It is but justice."

Justice! I laughed in his face. Justice that a man fighting for his life should also perish if, slaying one of his enemies, he himself still lived!

My laughter infuriated him. "Enough delay!" he cried impatiently. "Come, decide! Go to them, or promise to obey! Death or life. Which? Do you promise?"

What a terrible choice I was offered? A horrible death beneath fangs of beasts which should never have existed, with no one ever to know that I had resisted the temptation of proffered life; or an even more terrible existence as one of these unnatural things, half man, half demoniac beast! But if I chose death, I should have a highly problematical hope of future life in the skies, and my wife and daughter would be left alone.

If I chose life, I should have high adventure to season my prosaic existence; I should have wealth with which I could buy a title. Besides, something might happen to save me from the fate which otherwise would sometime inevitably overtake me. Is it any wonder to you, why I chose as I did? Would you not do the same, in my predicament? Even if

I had it all to do over again, knowing what I now know, I think I should say again that which I answered the master: "I promise!"

But God! If I had only chosen death!

The things that I saw, heard, and did that night made a stain on my soul that all eternity will never erase. But finally they were over, and we separated, each returning to his home, and the master where no one knows.

I resumed my form by the tree, and as I did so, I remembered the events that had taken place that night. I fell prone on the grass, screaming, cursing and sobbing, to think of my fate to come. I was damned forever.

Although I have called myself a wampyr, I was not one in the true sense of the word, at the time of which I speak. Neither were any of the rest of my companions, except the master, for although we ate human flesh and drank blood, we did so to assuage our fierce hunger more than because it was necessary for our continued existence. We ate heartily of human food also, in the man form, but more and more we found it unsatisfying and came to possess a cannibalistic appetite which only flesh and blood would conquer.

Gradually we were leaving even this for a diet consisting solely of blood. This, in my firm belief, was that which the master lived upon. His whole appearance bore this out. He was incredibly aged, and I believe an immortal. He still may be, for no one has seen him dead, although they tell me that he is.

His face was like a crinkled, seamed piece of time-worn parchment, coal black with age. His eyes glittered with youth, seeming to have almost a separate existence of their own. Gradually, very gradually, the expressions of our faces were changing also, and we were turning into true wampyrs when self-brought catastrophe overtook us.

I will not dwell long upon the year or so in which I was the master's slave, for our dark and bloody deeds are too

35

numerous to mention in detail. Some nights we wandered about in fruitless search and returned empty handed, but usually we left death and destruction behind us. Most times, however, we would be summoned on some definite foray, which culminated in each of us being, the next day, somewhat richer.

On one occasion when we dragged down humans, my conscience has always rested easily. We had set out on the track of a sleigh loaded with wealthy travelers from foreign parts; an old man and his two grandsons about three to five years of age. We followed for several miles to find the sleigh lying on its side, the horses gone, and the three travelers stiff and stark on the dark stained snow, which was churned by many footprints of horse and man. Enraged not by the murder, for we ourselves had intended no less, but by the loss of our anticipated loot, we took up the trail which led away toward the mountains. Five men on horseback made up the party we followed. They spurred their horses to the utmost when we sang the Hunger Song, baying as we ran, but they were too slow for us. One by one, we pulled them down, slew the slayers and despoiled the thieves, which was a grim and ghastly jest.

But not often could I console myself thus. Many were the helpless and harmless that we removed from existence, and more horrible did we become. Day by day we were growing hardened and inured to our lot, and only rarely did my soul sicken as at my first metamorphosis.

CHAPTER III

Sometimes, when I walked the village streets, I had met people who seemed to glance furtively at me with a wild look. These glances were quickly averted, but by them I had begun to decide within myself just who were the other members of the pack. Growing bolder and more certain, I had accosted certain of them, to find myself correct.

One by one, I sounded them out, but found only Simon the smith to be of my own sentiments toward our gruesome business. The rest all exulted in the joyous hunt, and could not, we were certain, be persuaded to revolt against this odious enslavement.

But gradually, as we became more hardened and unprincipled, more calloused to the suffering we caused, we had become yet more greedy and rapacious. Here Simon and I found a loophole to attack.

As I have said before, the master never took any of the money, jewels or other portable valuables which we found on the bodies or amongst the possessions of those whom we slew.

So I dropped a word here, a hint there, a vague half-question to one individual singly and alone, while Simon did the same. The gist of all our arguing was, "What does the master take?"

This was a very pertinent question, for it was obvious to all of them that the master was not leader for nothing. He obtained something from each corpse when we went to it, alone, and we sat in the circle waiting eagerly for the signal to rush in.

To me it was plain that this was nothing more material than the life blood of the slain unfortunates, which kept the master alive! Simon and I said nothing of this, gradually forming the opinions of the others to the effect that the immortal souls were absorbed into the master's being, giving him eternal life.

This staggering thought opened great possibilities in the minds of most, and as we thought, all; later I was to learn to my sorrow that not all were so credulous. But more and more they became dissatisfied, less patiently did they restrain themselves from leaping in ahead of their turn, on our bandit raids. For working in their minds, like worms in carrion, or smoldering sparks in damp cloth, which will presently burst into flame, was this: "Why not be immortal myself?"

So were discord and revolt fomented, and so was I the unwitting cause of my further undoing, and, strangely, my redemption.

Now, my wife was a good woman, and I am sure that she loved me as much as I loved her, but this very love worked our ruin. All people have a weakness in one way or another, and she was no exception to the rule. She was jealous—insanely jealous!

My frequent absences, which I thought had been unnoticed, since I had been careful not to make the slightest noise in opening the window and quitting the house, had been observed for weeks.

I found later that one had told the master what Simon and I had started, and it was the only female member of our pack. But he had already perceived, with his cunning senses, the almost imperceptible signs of revolt against his absolute power. Determining to crush this at the start, he decided to make an example of someone to bind the rest more closely to him by means of a new fear.

Why he chose me instead of Simon, I have not the faintest idea, unless it was that I was more intelligent than the ignorant clods that made up the rest of the pack. But so it was; I was chosen to be the victim, and this the way he set about to bind me forever to him.

He enlisted the aid of old Mother Molla, who was regarded as a witch that had sold her soul to the devil. How she got into the house I never was able to discover, for the original excuse was either forgotten later, or merely left untold. But to the house she came one day, probably obtaining an entrance on some flimsy pretext of begging for cast-off clothing, or of borrowing some cooking utensil.

Before she left she casually mentioned that she had seen me in the early morning before sunrise, coming past her hut. There were only two houses in that part of the wood, Mother Molla's and the charcoal burner's, whose name was Fiermann. All would have yet been well, but the old hag insinuated that Fiermann had a young and pretty daughter, and that he himself was in town very often over night. And so the seeds suspicion were planted in my wife's mind.

She said that she ordered the hag out, and helped her across the threshold with a foot in her back, and when the old witch picked herself out of the mud, she screamed to my wife, "Look for yourself, at half an hour before midnight," and hobbled away cackling to herself.

The mischief was done. At first my wife resolved to think nothing about the matter, but it preyed on her mind and gnawed at her heart. So, to ease her suspicions, she worked away a knot in the partition; and that night when I had gone to bed, she waited and watched.

She saw me fling back the clothes and step out of bed, fully dressed, then walk silently across the floor and open

39

the window, to vanish carefully into the moonlit night. At first, she told me later, she was horrified and heartbroken to think me unfaithful; then she resolved to go away or kill herself, so she would not be a hindrance to me any longer. But finally her emotions changed and vanished until only hate was left. She resolved to watch and wait to see what might befall. She sat by the knothole until I came back just as the cock crowed; then she went to bed herself, to toss about sleeplessly until morning.

Night after night she waited, sometimes fruitlessly, for it was not every night that the silent call summoned us to the rendezvous. But when, in a period of three weeks, I had stealthily stolen out eight times, and she had satisfied herself that Fiermann had also been away with artful questions to his girl, her suspicions were confirmed. He was with the pack, but neither knew that. So she decided to confront me with the facts and tell me to choose between the two.

All this time the master's mind was working upon hers to such effect that, although she thought she was choosing her own course of action, in reality she was following the plans which the master had made for her.

One night I heard the silent howl which never failed, when I was in the man form, to send a chill down my back. I had been expecting this for several days, and had remained dressed each night until midnight, to be in readiness for the summons.

I stepped carefully to the window and released the catch that held it down, then lifted. It stuck! I tugged harder with no better results.

Well, then, I should have to use the door. It was dangerous, but might be done. At all means, anything was preferable to going wild within the house. So I turned and was struck fairly in the eyes by a splinter of yellow light. Someone was on the other side of the partition door with a lighted candle, and the door was slowly opening.

40

Instantly I knew that I was discovered. I bounded toward the bed, intending to simulate sleep until she had gone away, but the door flew open with a crash, and my wife stood in the doorway with a scornful look on her face, and a candle held high, which cast its rays upon me. It was too late to hope for escape, so I attempted to brazen it out.

"Well, what is it?" I asked gently.

"What were you doing at the window?" she said.

"It is so hot in here that I thought to let some air in," I replied.

"To let air in, or yourself out?" came, though spoken in a low tone, as a thunderclap to me.

I was struck dumb, and then she told me the whole story as she knew it. The mass of lies with which old Molla must have started her mind in a ferment poured into my consciousness in a heap of jumbled words.

Again came the howling cry, that only I could hear, and I thought I detected a note of anger in it.

"At first," she said, "I did not believe, but when I saw with my own eyes—"

"Silence!" I roared with such vehemence that the window rattled.

"I will be heard!" she cried. "I have nailed down the window and you shall not pass through this door tonight."

She slammed the door, and stood dauntlessly before it! My heart went out to her in this moment. That bright little figure, standing there so bravely, made me forget why I must go. I took a step toward her—and that long eery wail, which only re-echoed in my brain, sounded much more wrathfully—and nearer.

Torn between two desires, I stood still. My face must have been a mask of horror and anguish, for she looked at me in amazement, which softened to pity.

"What is it, dear?" she whispered. "Have I wronged you after all?"

Then I felt the pangs of change beginning and knew that

41

the transformation would follow quickly. I seized a heavy stool and flung it through the window, following it as quickly myself. If I was to escape, not a second could be wasted.

With a swiftness I had never dreamed she possessed, she ran to me as I crouched in the window with my hands on the side, and one knee on the sill, drawing myself up and over.

She seized me by the hair and dragged my head back, crying meanwhile, "No, no! You shall not go. You are mine, and I shall keep you!"

Then she pulled so mightily that I fell upon my back. All was lost! It was too late, for I no longer had any desire to leave! Although I still maintained the outward appearance of a man, I thought as a beast.

I have often though that the change first took place in the brain and later in the body. I shrieked demoniacally, and another cry arose outside the house, sounding loud through the broken window.

She paled at the sound and shrank back against the table, terrified at my wild and doubtless uncanny appearance. I sprang to my feet, tearing madly at my clothes, ripping them from my body in pieces. I had all the terror of a wild animal now for encumbering clothing or anything like a trap.

When completely stripped, I howled again loudly, and fell upon all fours, a misshapen creature that should never have existed. I had become a wild beast! But it was not I, who slunk bellying the floor, hair all abristle with hate, toward the horror stricken figure by the table; it was not I—I swear before the God that soon will judge me!

At a sound outside, I turned, standing astride my victim, and ready to fight for my kill.

With forepaws on the window sill, through the broken pane a wolf's head peered. With hellish significance, it glanced at the door of the next room, wherein lay our

42

little girl, asleep in her cradle. The eyes turned upon me in mute command.

It was I, the man spirit, who for a moment ruled the monstrous form into which my body had been transmuted. It was the man, myself, who curled those thin, beastly lips into a silent, menacing grin, who stalked forward, stiff-legged, hackles raised and eager for revenge!

As swiftly as the head had appeared, it withdrew. Suddenly it appeared again, curiously changing in form. The outlines grew less decided, and everything seemed to swim before my eyes. I grew giddy, and there visibly the wolf's head changed into that inscrutable parchment mask of the master. Those youthful eyes glared balefully into mine, with a smoky flame behind them.

I felt weak; again the beast was in the ascendant, and human heritage was forgotten. Lost, too, was all memory of love or revenge. I, the werewolf, slunk through the door, over to the cradle, gloatingly stood anticipating for a moment while the blood dripped from my parted jaws. Then I clamped down my jaws on her dress, and heedless of her puny struggles or cries, I rose with a long clean leap through the broken window.

After that, to my tortured memory comes one of those curious blank spots that sometimes afflicted me. I dimly remember the snarls of fighting animals, and, more strangely, the sounds of shots, but who could be wandering about at that time of night, armed with so untrustworthy a weapon?

Soon, we were roaring down the valley with the master before the hellpack. Foam from bloody jaws flecked the snow with pink as we galloped along, mounting the hill like a wave breaking on the beach. We were racing along at full speed with the master still ahead and the rest of the pack strung out at varying distances behind, when suddenly he turned in midleap, and alighting, confronted us.

The one who was directly in front of me, and behind the master, dug his feet into the ground and slid in order to avoid collison. I was going so swiftly I could not stop, and piled up on my mate. The next instant we were at the bottom of a struggling, clawing, snapping heap. For a moment we milled and fought, while the master sat on his haunches, and lolled his tongue out of gaunt grinning jaws, breath panting out in white, moist puffs.

Then we scattered as if blown apart, and also settled into a resting position, a very sheepish looking pack of marauders. At that moment, I felt taking place within me the tearing, rending sensation that always preceded the transforming of our bodies from one form to another. My bones clicked into slightly different positions; I began to remember that I was human, and stood erect, a man again.

All of my companions had been transformed likewise, and were standing where they had stopped.

What a contrast! Six men, white men, each a giant in strength, bound till death and after, bound to a thing which I cannot call a man. A creature of only four feet high, which physically the weakest of us might have crushed with one hand. But six men were slavishly obedient to his every order, and moved in mortal fear of him. The pity of it! Only two of us were still human enough to understand that we were damned forever and had no means of escape. To look at their faces made that plain, for deeply graven there were lines that brutalized them, making out swift progress toward the beast.

I was changing also. I had been told frequently how bad I looked, and my friends thought I should rest more, for it was plain that I was overtaxing my energies; but I always changed the subject as soon as possible, for I knew the real reason of my appearance.

But now the master was advancing. An irresistable force urged me toward him, and as I moved the others closed in about me, so that he and I stood in the center of a small circle.

"Comrades," he leered at me as he spoke, and I grew hot with rage, but said nothing. "I have gathered you here

44

with me this night to give you a warning that you may use for your own profit. Leave me to do as I see fit and all will be well, but try for one instant to change my course of action or to attack me, and you will curse the day you were born."

Then he lost control of himself.

"Fools!" he shrilled. "Cursed, peasant fools; you who thought you could kill me whom even the elements cannot harm! Idiots who tried to plot against the accumulated intelligence of a thousand years, listen to me."

Thunderstruck at this sudden outburst, we staggered and reeled under the revelation which came next.

"From the very first," he cried, "I saw through your stupid intrigue against me, and I laughed to myself. Every move you made, every word you spoke in the seeming privacy of your hovels, I knew long before you. This is nothing new to me. Many times has this been tried upon me, and many times have I met the problem in exactly the same way. I have made an example of one of you to warn the rest, and there he stands?"

He whirled swiftly and thrust an ash-gray claw at my face. For some time I had been realizing now what he was about to say, and at this sudden blow I averted my eyes from his and sprang at his throat.

We went down together, and he would have died there and then, but they tore us apart. Poor, blind fools! Again he stood erect, rubbing his throat where I had clutched it, and again he croaked, never glancing at me, as I was held powerless by three men.

"All of you have children, wives, or parents dependent upon you. I saw to that before I chose you, having this very thing in mind. I can at any time change any one of you to a beast by the power of my will, wherever I may be. Tomorrow, if you still resist me I will change you, or you," he said, darting his paw at each in quick succession.

From the circle rose cries of "No! No! Do not do that! I

am your man," and "Master, you are our father; do with us as you like!"

Triumphant, he laughed, there in the snowy plain beneath the starry sky, then bent his gaze upon me. Seizing my chin, he forced my eyes to meet his, and growled. "And you? What say you now?"

I could not resist those burning eyes.

"Master," I muttered. "I am your willing slave."

"Then get back to your den," he cried, giving me a push that sent me prone in the snow. "Wait there until I summon you again."

The pack changed from men to brutes, and raced off toward the forest. I tried to follow, but I could not move until the sound of their cries had faded away into the distance. Finally, I rose and went to my dreary home again.

I will pass over briefly what followed; I do not think I could repeat my thoughts as I stumbled along through the night, nearly freezing from lack of clothing and the exposure that resulted.

Dawn was arriving when I came in sight of the four walls I had so recently called home. I staggered in and sank into a chair, too listless to build a fire.

After a while, mechanically, I dressed myself, started a blaze in the fireplace, and bethought myself of hiding the body, which lay in the other room, until I could flee. Plan after plan suggested itself to my mind, but all were soon cast aside as useless. Tired out, I buried my head on my arms as I sat by the table, and must have dozed away some little time.

Suddenly, I was aroused from the dull apathy into which I had fallen by a timid knock on the door. My first thought was that I was discovered. A fit of trembling overcame me, and although it quickly passed, it left me too weak to rise.

Again sounded the rap, followed by the rasp of frosty

gravel as footsteps haltingly passed down the clean swept path.

Suddenly, a plan had formulated itself in my poor distracted brain. I steeled my will to resolute action, hastened to the door, and threw it wide. No one was in sight.

Bewildered, I looked about, suspicious of more wizardry, and between two of the trees that fringed the road I spied a figure slowly traveling toward the village.

"Hai!" I shouted, cupping my hands at my mouth. "What do you want? Come back!"

As the figure turned and approached me, I recognized the half-witted creature who limpingly traveled from village to village during the summer months, working when compelled by necessity to do so, but more often begging his food and shelter from more fortunate people.

"Why do you knock at my door?" I asked, as kindly as I could, when he had come near to me.

"I came last evening," he said. "The lady that lives here said that she was alone and would not let me in or give me anything, but if later I would come when her husband had returned, she would let me have some old clothes and something good to take with me. So I slept with cows, and now I am come again."

I forced myself to speak composedly.

"You are a good lad, and if you will do something for me, I will see that you receive new clothing and much money. Here is proof that I mean well," and I tossed a broad gold piece to his feet.

Wildly did he scramble in the dust of the path, but I had no mood to laugh, ridiculous as his action would have seemed at another time. He whimpered in his eagerness to be off, looked into my face, and cowered as does a dog that expects a blow.

Some of my agony of spirit must have been reflected in my face, for he shrank away. All his joy vanished, and he faltered fearfully. "What would you have me do, master?"

His pitiable aspect struck to my heart, and the words I

47

had been about to speak died still-born on the end of my tongue. I shall never reveal to anyone what my intention had been, but something nobler and purer than I had ever known enlivened my soul. I drew myself to my full height, glared defiantly at the quivering wretch and cried, "Go you to Ponkert. Arouse the people and bring the soldiers from the barracks. I am a werewolf and I have just slain my wife!"

His eyes seemd starting from his head, his nerveless and palsied limbs carried him shakily down the path, the while he watched me over his shoulder as if he expected to see me turn into a wolf and ravenously pursue him. At the end of the path, he bethought himself of flight, threw the gold piece down and started with a curious, reeling run toward the village.

A little wind was now rising, blowing flurries of snow and leaves about, and the round evil eye of yellow metal lay and blinked at the morning sun until a little whirlwind of dust collapsed on it and buried its gleam. But although I could not see it I knew it was there. The thing that all men slave, war and die for, that all men desire, and obtaining are not satisfied, the struggle for which has maimed and damned more souls than any other one thing that has ever been. I went it, shut the door, and left it outside in the dirt, whence it came and where it belongs.

It might have been a minute or a year that I sat at the table, with my head buried in my arms, for any memory that I have of it. But so I found myself when I was roused by a dull roar of many voices outside. Opening the door, I stepped out and waited, expecting nothing less than instant death.

A crowd of about fifty persons came surging up the road, and seeing me standing there, passively waiting, milled and huddled together, each anxious to be in at the death, but caring not to be in the forefront and first to meet the dreaded werewolf.

48

Much coaxing and urging was given certain of the crowd to send them to me, but none was eager for fame.

Finally, one tanner stepped out, clad only in his leather apron, and carrying a huge fish spear in his right hand.

"Come," he shouted. "Who follows if I lead?"

From far down the road came the pounding of hoofs.

"He who comes must hasten," thought I, "if he would see the finish."

The tanner harangued the steadily growing mob without avail, none desiring to be the first.

At last I was out of the common rut in which the rest of the village was sunken. What a moment! Even in my hopeless situation I could not help but exult. Seventy-five or one hundred against one, and not a man dare move!

At last the tanner despaired of assistance and slowly moved toward me, now and then casting a glance behind to be assured of an open lane of retreat if such was necessary.

I believe, in that moment, that had I leapt forward at them, the whole flock of sheep would have fled screaming down the road; but I did nothing of the kind. I did not move, or even make any resistance when the tanner seized me by the shoulder, his spear ready for the deadly stroke. Why should I? Life had no longer any interest for me!

Finding that I stood passively, the tanner released my shoulder, grasped the spear in both hands, and towered above me, his mighty muscles standing out like ropes on his naked arms and chest. The whole assemblage held its breath for the silence was that of death. A loud clatter of hoofs twitched every head around as if they all had been worked simultaneously by a single string. Straight into the crowd, which broke and scattered before it, came a huge, black horse, ridden by a large man in the uniform of the king's soldiery. As he came, he smote right and left with the flat of his long straight sword.

Down came the spear, and down swept the sword full upon the tanner's head. He fell like a poleaxed steer, while

49

the spear buried itself for half its length in the ground by the door.

"This man is mine!" he shouted. "Mine and the king's! He must go with me for trial and sentence; touch him at your peril."

The crowd murmured angrily, started for us, but disintegrated again before the rush of half a company of soldiers that had followed their captain.

CHAPTER IV

"And so, sirs," I was concluding my narrative in the prison barracks at Ponkert, "you see to what ends have I been brought by the machinations of this creature. I do not ask for life myself, for I shall be glad to die, and it is but just that I should; but give me revenge, and I will burn in hell for eternity most happily."

For a time, I thought that the officer would deny me, for he ruminated long before he spoke.

"Can you," he said, "entrap this hideous band, if my men and I will give you help?"

I leaped from my chair and shouted, "Give me a dozen men, armed, and not one of those fiends will be alive tomorrow morning!"

Carried away by my enthusiasm, he cried, "You shall have fifty, and I will lead them myself." But then, more gravely, "You realize that we cannot leave one alive? That all must die? All?"

I nodded and looked him squarely in the eyes.

"I understand," I said. "When we have won, do with me as you will. I shall not resist, for I am very tired, and shall be glad to rest. But until then, I am your man!"

'You are brave," he said simply, "and I wish I need not do that which I must. Will you grip hands with me before we leave?" he asked, most diffidently.

I said nothing, but our hands met in a strong clasp, and as he turned away I thought I saw moisture fleck his cheek. He was a man, and I wish I had known him earlier. We could have been friends, perhaps.

Some distance from Ponkert there stands a wood so dense that even at midday there in the center of the forest, only a dim twilight exists. Here sometimes laired the pack. At night, we had made it our meeting place, and now and again, in the thickest recesses, one or more of us would spend the day in seclusion. So, knowing this, I made my plans.

I tore my clothes, and dabbled them in blood, wound a bloody bandage around my head, and the soldiers tied my hands securely behind me, also putting a chord about my neck.

Toward evening we set out, about eighty of us in all, including the rusties who trailed along behind, carrying improvised arms—hay forks, clubs, and farm implements, which were clumsy, yet deadly.

Straight through the heart of the wood we passed, I traveling, in the midst, reeling along with head down as if worn out, which indeed I was. Now and then, the soldier who held the other end of the cord would jerk fiercely, almost causing me to stumble, and on one of these occasions I heard a sullen, stifled growl from a thicket which we were passing. No one else apparently heard. I cautiously lifted my head, and saw a form slink silently into the darker shadows. I had been observed, and the plan was succeeding!

We then passed from the forest and came into the sunlight once more. Between the wood and the hills flowed the river that before had served me so ill. Overlooking this, there frowned a great castle that had once dominated the river and the trade routes which crossed the plain on the other side. But this was long ago; so long that the castle builders had passed away, their sons, and theirs also, if indeed there ever were such, leaving only the castle to prove they had ever lived.

As the years went on, various parties of brigands had held the great stone structure, and wars had been fought around and within. Slowly, time and the elements had worked their will, unchecked, until the central tower squatted down one day and carried the rest of the castle with it.

Still there remained a strong stone wall, which had enclosed the castle once, but now formed a great square, thirty feet in height, around a shapeless mountain of masonry in the center. Under this imposing monument lay the last who had ever lived there, and some say that their ghosts still haunt the ruins, but I never saw any, or met one who had. At each side of the square there stood an iron gate in the walls. These were still well preserved, but very rusty; so rusty indeed, that it was impossible to open them, and we were obliged to find an easier mode of entrance.

Finally, we discovered a large tree, which, uprooted by a heavy wind, had fallen with its top against the wall, and so remained, forming a bridge which connected the wall and the ground by a gentle incline.

To gain the courtyard it was necessary to follow the wall around to where it faced the plain. Here a large section had fallen inward, leaving the wall but twenty feet in height at that point. Here we went down, by the rope which had tormented me so, and prepared our trap.

It was very simple; I was the bait, and we knew that when the time for the change, they would follow my trail unless the master was warned. And once inside the walls they could not leap out. We could then slay them at our leisure, for we were more than ten to one, although many of the farmers had refused to enter the haunted castle and had returned to the village.

As midnight approached, I heard the cries, faintly and far away in the wood below.

"The time is near," I whispered to the captain, as we stood in the enclosure. "I hear them gathering."

"Be ready," he warned them. "Hide yourself in the rocks. They come!"

Eagerly, we waited. Nothing was visible now except the captain and two or three soldiers standing by the pile of masonry.

As I waited near a large pile of stone blocks, I heard someone cry sharply, "Now!"

Shooting lights danced before my eyes, followed by black oblivion, and I fell foward on my face. I had been clubbed from behind.

When I became conscious again the stars still gleamed brightly over head, but they no longer interested me. My sole thought was to escape from these two legged creatures that held me prisoner. Again I was the beast.

For the first time I had not been aware of the transition when it took place. Now I had no recollection of my past, and for all I knew I might never have been anything but a quadruped.

Came swiftly the realization that I was being called insistently. From the tail of my eye, I saw a man standing beside me, but a little distance away. Perhaps I might escape!

I drew my legs up, and my muscles tightened for the spring. I would leap the wall, I would flee for my life, I would . . . and then a tremendous weight came crashing down on my hind quarters, breaking both my legs.

The pain was excruciating! I gave vent to a scream of agony which was answered by howls of mingled encouragement and rage from beyond the wall. Then down from the wall came leaping, one at a time, five great, gray brutes. They had followed my trail and come, as they thought, to save me, not dreaming they were being led into a trap.

The soldiers had been wiser than I, for they had foreseen what I failed to see: that if my story was true, inevitably when my nature changed I would betray them to my comrades.

Between man and wild beast there can be no compromise, so they stunned me, and then toppled down a heavy stone, pinning me to the ground. Instead of warning the pack as I undoubtedly would have done had I but known earlier that they were present, I screamed for help, for the sudden pain drove any other emotion from my mind.

Now all was confusion. Howl of beast, and shout of man, mingled in chorus with clash of pike and fang. Now and again, but infrequently, a shot punctuated the uproar, but these new weapons are too slow to be of practical use.

The five were giving a far better account of themselves than I had dreamed possible. Springing in and out again with lightning movements, they could tear a man's throat out and be gone before he could defend himself. The confusion was so great, the press so thick, that a man might kill his comrade by accident. I saw this happen twice.

Now only four were visible, springing to and fro, fighting for their lives like cornered rats, and gradually forcing their way to the wall whence they had come. One must be down!

But no! I saw the missing one rending with sharp white fangs at something which lay half hidden beneath him. A soldier stole silently up behind, and with a mighty display of strength thrust a pike completely through the wolf's body. But other eyes than mine had seen the stroke. The next instant he went down and was buried from sight in the center of the snarling pack. Now the pack was, for several seconds, in a tight knot of bodies, and while they remained thus, the soldiers leaped in with pikes and clubs flailing. Before the stricken wolf had reached the corner toward which he was slowly crawling, coughing out his life in bloody bubbles, the remainder of the pack had joined him in death.

It was at this critical moment that a head peered over the

wall. Two bright little, red eyes took in the scene. Why the master had delayed his arrival until this time I cannot explain. But whatever his faults, he was at least no coward, for the first inkling the men had of his presence was the sight of the black wolf springing down and landing on the heap of dead bodies which had represented his former vassals.

With a bound he was in the midst of the soldiers, fighting with fang and claw. They scattered like sheep, but returned to form a close packed circle around him, barring all egress. Now his only chance of life lay in motion so swift that it would be unsafe to aim a weapon at him for fear of injuring one of the men.

He saw clearly that all was lost, and quite obviously perceived that flight was his only hope. He gave a glance of encouragement as I lay there raving and frothing, snapping at, and breaking my teeth upon, the cold unyielding rock that held me down; and he rushed madly about the inside of the circle, searching for a weak spot in it. In they pressed, striking now and then as he passed, but not harming him.

With hot, red tongue hanging from slavering jaws, he raced about the encircling cordon of foes. Soon was his plan of action made. He leaped in midstride straight at an ignorant yokel who wielded a hay fork. The poor fool struck clumsily, instead of dodging, and, missing, the mistake was his last. Instantly the master had torn out his throat with a single snap, and was streaking toward the castle wall.

Now the way was clear. Puffs of snow rose behind, before him, and on either side, but apparently he bore a charmed life for none of the missiles struck him. As he reached the wall, he left the ground in the most magnificent leap I have ever seen from either man or beast, hanging by his fore feet twenty feet above the ground for the space of time in which a man might count ten. And then, while bullets be-starred the ancient masonry all about him, he scrambled wildly with his hind feet to draw himself up, and was soon over the wall and gone.

They rushed to the rusted gate, but their very haste defeated their efforts. By the time they reached the open, the plain was bare of life. But over the hill to the eastward floated a derisive, mocking howl. The master's farewell! From that day to this he has never been seen in Ponkert. The rule of the wolf was ended.

Now my ordeal is ended, the master ousted, and the fear that held sway over the village finished. I, out of all the pack that ravaged the land for many miles, alone am left alive. Somewhere, perhaps, the master still roams silently, stealthily, in the cool darkness of our nights, but I am sure that never again will he return to Ponkert. This is my assurance.

When his power crumbled to dust in the courtyard of that ancient castle, and he was forced to flee for his life, his last look and cry to me intimated that he would return and rescue me from my captors. There must have been some spark of humanity in that savage heart, something that would not allow him to leave those who had sworn allegiance to him; for witness that magnificent leap from the courtyard wall to the very midst of his foes, to save the one surviving member of his band.

He did return!

While I lay in the barracks dungeon, recovering from my broken bones and other injuries, one night about a week after the fight I heard the old familiar, silent cry.

I recognized the master's call and responded. I thought of all things I should like to tell him and could not through the two feet of stone wall. I went over in my mind the whole series of actions by means of which I had escaped from his horrible enslavement.

Beginning with the involuntary murder of my wife and child, I related without uttering a spoken word that which I had done, and ended with the moment when I saw him leap the gap, a fugitive. I know he understood, for after

57

a few seconds of silence, just outside the wall there arose the blood chilling howl of a wolf. Higher and higher it rose, a long, sobbing wail of hate, and undulating crescendo of sound. It thinned to a thread whose throaty murmur was drowned in the rushing trample of heavy feet overhead, and the crash of exploding powder. Flash after flash tore the velvet night, mingling with the shouts of the soldiers who were firing from the windows. At some time during the tumult, the master turned his back on Ponkert for the last time, I trust.

Utterly alone in the world, friendless and forlorn, I quit tomorrow this mortal form that has known such strange changes.

I go with no reluctance whatever, for I have nothing to live for. They tell me that every pang I suffer now shall shorten my punishment in the future. What my pains on earth shall be, I know not. I may be broken on the wheel or stretched upon the rack, but I am resigned and fortified against my fate.

There is one thing of which I am positive, for they have told me to add pang upon pang. I shall be flayed alive, my hide tanned like a beast's, and my dark and gloomy history written upon it for all to read who can!

I have never heard of these things being done before, but I have no doubt that they will be done to me. However, I care not. So much have I suffered in heart and thought that no bodily discomfort can surpass my other torments. I am resigned. May he who reads take warning. Farewell to all whom I know and have known. Farewell!

*   *   *   *   *   *

When the manuscript was finished, I sat thinking for a little time. So this book was written on a human hide which, when occupied, had enclosed Pierre's ancestor.

"I thought," said I to the old man, "that you told me that the person described in the narrative was your grandfather many times removed. But here it relates that his only child was murdered by himself in beast form. How do you explain that?" I asked.

"You will remember, perhaps, that he told now, after the flight from the cottage, immediately succeeding the act was a blank, save for a vague remembrance of shots. What is more probable than that someone aroused by the howling in the night should fire blindly at the noise, not once but several times. Granted that, it is probable that, frightened by the unexpected noise, the beasts would leave their prey. Such is the legend that has accompanied the book for centuries. Also, it is said that this book has never been out of the possession of the Hungarian's descendants. Therefore, observing that I now possess the book which was given to me by my father, as it was to him by his parent, I assume that in my veins courses the diluted strain of the werewolf."

"This may all be true," I said. "Surely in the weeks of his imprisonment he must have been informed that his little girl had not been devoured; yet he speaks consistently as if he knew nothing about the rescue."

"Ah," he replied. "That puzzled me also, when I first heard of this. But it is my sincere belief that this information was kept purposely from him to add mental torture to his physical punishment. Why should they trouble themselves to ease the spirit of a man that was responsible for so many crimes?" And such a cruel glitter lit his eyes, that I had nothing more to say.

After I had left, I congratulated myself upon being so fortunate as to exist in the prosaic Twentieth Century, and not in the superstition-ridden ones which we have just barely left. For even superstitions must have a beginning, and who knows how much truth may lie, after all, in this weird tale?

I never went back to the inn after that. I often meant to, but other business was more important, and procrastination finally made the journey useless.

Pierre is dead now, leaving no relatives or friends but myself. I now possess the book, and it lies before me, as I write the story it contains for the world to read.

THE WEREWOLF'S

DAUGHTER

CHAPTER 1

A band of tired, dusty men, travelworn but gay, plodded down the road which led to Ponkert, as the swift summer night began to drop down upon Hungary.

In the barracks of the soldiers, who were quartered perhaps a mile from the village, scattered lights were shining, although the western sky was still red. The sentry that paced before the gate spat disgustedly on the ground as the men went by flinging cheerful gibes at one who was satisfied to risk life itself for hire when he might be his own master, free as the wind that blows through the forest.

He, in his turn, sneered at a folk too wild and unnatural to appreciate the comforts of a warm bed indoors, regular meals, and the joy of service to the country.

It was the age old quarrel of plainsman versus townsman, wanderer against stolid peasant; one of the solid backbone of the nation, the other its restless blood ever on the move.

There were many such roving bands in this period of unrest. The times were ripe for change, and one was coming even then, for on the watery desert of the Atlantic, three small ships plowed an uncharted sea—ships manned by the scum of the waterfronts of Palos and emptied prisons but which were a line flung from the Old World to the New, along which would flow news that would affect the destiny of countless yet unborn.

But now, Ponkert drowsed away among its surrounding hills, far enough from the Black Sea to be safe from the Turks with whom the country was sporadically at war; small enough to leave other communities in peace; and because the soil of that section was poor and stony, the people having little of value, they were not disturbed in their routine of life.

The wresting of food from the barren fields, squabbling in barter at the village shops, strolls at twilight by the riverside, devotion at the church; in such manner flowed the even current of their lives, pleasantly interrupted by an occasional caravan that passed through, such as now was on the border of the village. These wanderers were always welcome, for they brought news, a thing hardly come by, a breath of life to the stagnating community.

They were horse traders, traveling merchants, musicians of note, and their women were possessed of strange, magical powers. By these powers they could divine from the stars, a pool of ink, or the lines in a man's palm, what the future had in store for that man. And—most mysterious of all—anyone might enjoy these marvelous attainments for the price of a silver piece.

Their advent was borne before them on the wind which carried the squeal of ungreased cartwheels, the drone of foreign voices, the clank of horses' hoofs on stone, and the excited yapping of the dogs which followed the caravan. They were partly wolf, and the town dogs met them with bared fangs. A dozen fights would follow before they won through Ponkert, and the first wagon rolled into camp.

The wagons creaked and groaned into Ponkert, lurching wildly over the cobbled streets, the doughty little Tartar ponies straining every muscle on the unfamiliar footing. By the side of the wagons strode bronzed, bearded men of many races, but known by the general term of gipsies. Great, strapping fellows, hardly one over thirty, all showing mouthfuls of teeth in broad grins as they called to acquaintances among the townspeople, bandying coarse jests back and forth.

This was a band that had often passed through Ponkert, following a regular orbit of trade that swung through Germany, France, Italy, and on into the colder countries, completing its circle at the starting point in about two years. In all of these countries, the band had acquired new recruits, adventurers all, that longed for excitement and variety, or were called by the more prosaic lure of trade; so that faces of stolid, fair-haired Teutons were to be seen beside the dark countenances of the Latin races.

Mirko, the gipsy chieftain and a Pole, riding alone at the head of the caravan, dogweary but cockily twisting his long, black mustachios in order to create a terrifying aspect which would awe the natives, was suddenly aware of a drumming of hoofs in his rear.

Out of the tail of his eye he saw the nose and head of a magnificent bay creep up to his side, nostrils flaring as the animal changed its gait from a trot to a walk. Well aware of the newcomer's identity, he gave no sign that he had noticed the coming, only twisting his appendages the more.

These mustachios were the pride of Mirko's heart, and his greatest joy, for, hanging as they did like the tusks of a walrus, each full four inches long, they transformed his naturally benevolent face into an ugly mask. Mirko was a gentle soul, but there were few, even in his band, that realized it, because of his bluster, his wit, and his tremendous scowl. These had made him chief. The fiercest ruled in that desperate crew! So again, he preened his mustache and scowled his ugliest, looking straight ahead between his horse's ears.

A gentle, persuasive voice spoke to him. "How long in this village, Mirko?"

65

The chief grunted and turned around. "You, eh? I thought so. No one else would be addlepate enough to run his horse to death after it had traveled fifty miles since morning."

The boy grinned and wagged his finger reprovingly at his leader. "Ah, Mirko! What language to use to a poor fellow who came to visit because he thought you looked lonesome!"

Audacious speech to one as powerful as a gipsy chief, but Mirko loved the lad for it, and his mock scowl vanished in spite of himself.

"Never been able to fool you, have I?" he said cautiously, looking back to see if any of the following troops were in earshot.

These two were friends. When Mirko had first met Gunnar, the young Frenchman was wandering alone in Russia in search of adventure. His only weapon had been a bandura or three stringed violin, with which he sang like any troubadour for his supper, and a short dagger with which he carved that supper and his enemies alike. Mirko's heart warmed to the young daredevil so far from home, and he invited him to become a member of the band. The wanderer accepted with alacrity, being ever on the lookout for new experiences. Since that time, they had covered many a weary mile together, and Mirko loved the boy like a son. Hugo Gunnar set his cap askew with a slap of his hand, gave his embryonic mustache a fillip, and, ready for fight or frolic in the new encampment, he repeated his question.

"How long?" said the chief. "Three days, perhaps. Not more; less, I hope. We must be in Nizhni Novgorod for the great fair, and already we are far behind our plans. There's a sight for you, boy, when we get you back in Russia! Thousands of people, tents, shows, monsters, wrestling, bearbaiting, tame wolves, freaks, horse races! You'll never forget it. And the girls! Ah, Hugo, the girls! Every pretty girl in Russia goes to Nizhni Novgorod at fair time." Mirko

66

smacked his lips. "We will have to buy some new clothes for you. Nothing like gay feathers at mating time!"

"Bah!" broke in Gunnar. "You know I am not interested in girls. Chatter, chatter like rooks all day long, and when they have finished, nothing has been said."

"Not interested—Hugo, are you ill?" the chief asked solicitously, but with a crinkle about his thin mouth. "Why, boy, you're not human! Now when I was your age, I . . ." but here came a clattering interruption of hoofs, and Mirko bit his words short. His face resumed its usual saturnine scowl, and he snarled viciously at the intruder.

Only a trifling matter of a lost colt, but Mirko flew into a towering rage and had to go back personally to see that the search for it was undertaken at once. And Hugo Gunnar left alone at the head of the caravan.

Although they had passed through the town, he was very appreciative of the honor and sat straight in the saddle, now and then glancing to left and right, filled with a hope that people would believe him chief.

They had left Ponkert a mile behind, with a forest to their left and a few scattered cottages dotted among cultivated fields upon their right. The camp ground was not far, when Gunnar, allowing his glance to rove carelessly over the nearest of the buildings to see if anyone was watching, saw upon a rude porch a girl standing there. She was looking at him intently, and their glances met and clung.

With that meeting, soul spoke to soul, and each, in a second's time, felt a sudden surge of emotion.

The riders behind reached the youth and passed him, some grinning, others frowning, but all with crossed fingers as they neared the cottage. When they rode before him, shutting off his view of the lovely girl, cheeks now beginning to crimson at his steady gaze, he scowled, making aimless gestures with one hand as a man does to drive away an annoying fly which buzzes by his face as he reads. A warm, strange glow of happiness filled his being as he looked.

Her hair was chestnut brown and curled just enough to form a natural wave that his fingers yearned to stroke. Her eyes were dark, but color in them he could not distinguish, for her long lashes hid them. Her nose had that slight tilt which makes even an ordinary face adorable, but hers was no ordinary face.

At a later time, he saw that there were a very few, small freckles lightly sprinkled here and there like sun-kissed flower dust. But the mouth did not agree with the rest of her perfect features. The corners drooped and cast a sad, forlorn look over the sweet face. It was a mouth that had smiled very little in her life, and suddenly it came to him that it would be worth anything he possessed if he could make that face light up with pleasure and hear her laugh.

So lovely she looked, yet so sad and sorrowful, so cuddlesome for someone's strong arms, yet so obviously unwanted by anyone; for one who is loved does not have that dejected air. But now her eyes were shining, her lips half parted, as they gazed at one another, oblivious of their surroundings, not noticing that there was any other person on earth except themselves, though men were shouting and urging their beasts, wagons creaking dismally, and the dust of the road rolling high between them.

Gunnar felt a blow upon his shoulder, and a dig in the ribs. A jovial voice bellowed in his ear, "Aha, Hugo! Caught at last! Not interested in girls, eh? When they fall, they fall hard; but who is the fair one?" and Mirko squinted through the clouds of dust. Then his face paled beneath the grime.

"White Christ!" he croaked, and crossed himself with unaccustomed fingers, his banter slipping from him like a cloak. "The witch! Come away, quickly! She will put a spell on you, boy!" And he struck Hugo's horse a blow on the haunch that set him moving.

Hugo had been conscious that the horse had stopped, yet fully two thirds of the caravan had passed him while he sat staring at the sad girl, and now, while he and Mirko galloped on to their former place, he turned in his saddle for one last look, but the door of the cottage was shut, and she was gone. Riding once more at the head of the caravan, Mirko explained the terror that hung over her, and why she was feared by all in Ponkert.

The caravan swung to the left about the forest before he finished, and, to a question, he replied, "Her foster father is an old and grizzled giant, a marvel with the broadsword. This is all that has saved her from the peasants of this accursed village. They fear him, so they hardly dare to look at her. But when he dies, her life will not be worth that!"

He snapped his fingers, and the horse he rode took on a swifter gait, just as they entered a green clearing in the forest. Park-like it was, and spacious, and in its center bubbled up a clear spring of sweet water. By the time the two horses had drunk in the pool, the first wagon was rolling into the camp ground and the band was at home again for the night, one of many homes, and for many, the only home they knew.

CHAPTER II

To the girl upon the porch, as she stood watching the tired caravan plod down the road, a voice from inside the cottage had spoken.

She turned and closed the door, walking with the easy swing of a young panther to the chair where the old man sat and waited for her.

There was about him a certain dignity that hangs about one who is used to commanding and being instantly obeyed. In person, he was huge, with large, hairy hands and tremendously muscled arms depending from broad, strong shoulders. His waist tapered and was lean, and above was great depth of lung. His head was large and crowned with a mass of iron gray hair. His leonine face was gaunt and bony, with lines of patient suffering about his mouth. Now the deep set eyes glowed with pleasure as the girl came toward him, and a greeting rumbled from his cavernous chest.

"More gipsies, Ivga?" he asked.

"Yes, father," she answered, a fond note in her voice as she smiled at him with a look of adoration. "Many of them this time."

The old man sighed. "Bound for the fair, I suppose. Well, some day you and I will go, dear—when my legs are well."

He smoothed the blanket that swathed his knees. For a year he had not taken a step, a paralysis of the limbs rendering him helpless. There were grave doubts that he would ever walk again, but the girl had never been allowed to suspect that the ailment was other than temporary, and she looked forward to the time when they should stroll again by the river and through the forests.

She placed another stick upon the irons in the fireplace, and a row of crackling began as the flames seized it. While she stared into the fire, the crippled giant spoke again: "Bring me my sword, Ivga, if you will."

From its pegs above the fireplace, she lifted down the massive weapon, peeled back the soft leather casing that covered it, and laid it across his knees.

It was a beautiful sword, a double edged instrument of death, as sharp as Roland's sword Durandal, and on its five feet of blue steel was one word of gold inlay: Gate-Opener.

It had opened, in fact, many gates, both material and spiritual, being a crusader's sword that had hammered before the portal of Acre, swung again in the taking of the Holy City and in other battles, proving itself a gate-opener indeed between this world and the next.

In Dmitri, the sword of unknown history and age had found one who could wield it as it deserved, for although many owners had gripped it in battle since those roaring days and the ribbed, black hilt was now smooth, it was too ponderous to be used as other than a two handed sword for most men. And the day of such swords was nearly over.

Dmitri, with his strong right arm, had brandished it like an ordinary saber, smashing by brute force through those that opposed him. In crossing the room, Ivga, strong as she was, staggered beneath the weight of it.

When Dmitri moved his arms in the polishing, the cloth that covered them bulged with the play of his muscles. Often in fun, before his legs failed him, he would stand upright, thrust out his sword arm and dare her to bring it down if she could. And, though she hung from it by her hands with her full weight, feet drawn up and not touching the floor, it would be minutes before the arm came down. Such was the giant's strength.

His pleasures during his year of illness were few: the sight of Ivga, ever busied with his comfort; rude woodcarving to kill the time which hung so heavily upon him; the rare visits of some of the soldiers that he had commanded in years before; and last but greatest joy, the sharpening of his beloved sword.

A half dozen times a day he would labor upon its keen edge, sharpening it over and over until, like the fabled sword of Roland, it might almost have severed a pillow of down that floated upon water driven by the wind against its keen edge. Yet, as Roland was dissatisfied with the keenness of his sword, recasting it until it would sever three pillows, so Dmitri labored in perpetual employment upon Gate-Opener's edge, breathing upon some fancied spot of rust on the mirror surface, then dropping the polishing rag to sharpen a roughness that no one else could see, never admitting that there was such a thing as utter perfection. For then his chief delight would be over, and he loved this heavy blade that could cut through bone like cheese.

This day, he stroked the whetstone along its edge with soft, loving movements, the thin whispering from the razor edge as though Gate-Opener answered its master's low crooning in some metallic language which only they two could understand.

To him, laboring at his endless task of love, she came with a query on her lips and with worried, perplexed eyes. She came listlessly across the room, dropped upon her knees beside his chair, and laid a cool hand upon his wrist as he vigorously plied again the polishing rag.

"Father," she said, as he looked up, "Why do people hate me so?"

"Hate you, child?" Dmitri smiled. "No one hates you."

"They do," she insisted. "Everyone hates me. When I go down into the village, all of them look at me so strangely that it makes me feel afraid, and I come home as soon as I can."

"How do they look at you?" asked Dmitri, a little vein on each temple commencing to throb, and, unnoticed by either, the whetstone fell to the floor.

"Slyly, out of the corners of their eyes when I pass, and they edge far away from me if they can. Then sometimes after I have gone by, they make this sign and spit upon the ground behind me. Even the gipsies today—"

Here she closed the second and third fingers of her right hand into the palm and held them down with the thumb, thus making with the index and little finger the sign of the Horns, a charm still used in some countries against the evil eye.

"What does it mean?"

Dmitri ignored the question. "Do they ever say anything to you?" he gritted.

"No," she hesitatingly replied. "Not to me, but I have heard some say 'Witch' under their breath as I passed."

"By God! If I had my strength!" exclaimed the cripple, passionately. His knuckles whitened as his hands clenched on the chair arms. Breathing hard, his whole body trembling, he half rose, but the exertion was too much; his paralyzed limbs refused to bear his weight, and he fell back into the chair where he rested for a few moments with eyes shut.

The girl, alarmed by his silence, was about to speak, when he said in a lifeless tone, "How long have they acted so toward you, Ivga?"

"About a year, but they always shunned me ever since I can remember."

"But they have been more open since I became sick? More insulting?"

"Yes, father," the girl confessed.

"So," he muttered, half to himself, "when the lion is

73

caged the dogs grow bold. Well, Ivga, best stay indoors for a while until my legs get better, and then we'll leave this place. Ponkert? Pesthole!" He laughed shortly. "Keep away from the town. Stay here or near by where I can see you. None shall touch you here. I think I can promise you that."

His face set into hard, sinister lines that his soldiers of old would have recognized as his fighting face.. but which frightened the girl who had never seen the terrible look that he now wore.

"But why do they hate me?" she sobbed. "I never harmed them or anything belonging to them. I would love them all, everybody, if they would only let me. Nobody loves me but you; nobody ever has. No one would play with me when I was little. The games would break up if I tried to join. No one but you has ever taken me for boat rides on the river, or for walks or picnics in the Old Forest."

"Weren't you happy so, little daughter?" Dmitri asked sadly. "I tried to make you happy."

"Yes, I was—then, but now I want to be loved by other people, too. I want to be liked—I want to be loved because I am myself, and not because I am your daughter. I don't want everyone to hate me when I have done nothing to hurt them. Oh, I would love anybody—anybody, so much, if they would treat me kindly just a little bit! But everyone hates me so. I don't know what I want, but I am so lonesome that I feel as though I ought to be dead!"

"I should have known!" the cripple groaned in remorse. "I was a fool to try living in this village. I have spoiled your life, Ivga. Can you forgive me?"

"There is nothing to forgive, father. Why should I?" She lifted a tear-wet face to him. "See, I am smiling! I didn't mean it, really I didn't. I don't mind these people. They are nothing to me, but don't make me stay inside, penned in like an animal. I couldn't stand it. I must be free. I should die!"

"You may die, if you don't stay in," he groaned. "These

74

dogs yelp first, then bite, and I—I am helpless to protect you. Ivga, I am not your father, but I command you by the love you say you feel for me to stay close by. Danger is coming near to us."

"Not my—" the girl began, in a dazed tone, but Dmitri interrupted with a quick gesture.

"Wait!" he said. "I will tell you everything. I should have done so long ago, but I could not bear to do it. They hate you, and now I believe it must be a hate because they fear you."

"Fear me?" The girl laughed. "I only wish they did. If I were big and strong like you, father, I might make them fear me. But why should they be afraid of a little girl like me? And why hate me?"

"They hate you because they fear you," the cripple repeated. "All men hate the thing they fear, because they are ashamed of fear and deny that they are afraid, even to themselves. Still, they do fear, and sometimes they remove the cause of that fear. If it is an animal, they cage or tame it. If it is a poisonous weed or fruit or snake, they avoid or destroy it. If it is a man, they slay him. And they, all of them in this village of Ponkert, are afraid of you."

As she was about to interrupt, he stopped her. "Don't, Ivga. I will tell you a story that I should have told you long ago, and think not too hardly of me because you never knew before. You see, I thought you were happy, and I love you so I could not bear to hurt you. I love you with all a father's love, but I am not your father. I am a Czech, hired by good King Matthias, the first really brave king Hungary has ever had. Many of us came here to fight for him, and as we were dressed in black armor, we called ourselves the Fekete Seres—The Black Brigade. Some of us were quartered here when we first noticed your father, who was a native born Hungarian.

"Fifteen years ago, almost to a day, a beggar came running down this road with news for me. Terrible news it was, of how a jeweler had become a werewolf, a thing neither beast nor man, and had slain his wife while in the wolf shape, and, repentant, awaited someone to slay him in turn.

"Quick with the information, I had my horse saddled, and, with a half troop of my riders following, set out to save the man. It would have been a great deed for me to bring a werewolf, alive, before the king.

"The werewolf, though often spoken of, is rarely seen. One meets many a man who says that a friend of his has seen and fought with one, but it always turn out that this friend got his information from another friend, and so on. I expected, therefore, to gain promotion if I brought a real werewolf to the court, but I never did. Could I walk today, I would still be a captain and no more. The poor beggar, like the fool he was, stopped in the village before he came to me.

"It was ten miles to the village from the werewolf's house, and he might have hoped that someone would buy him a drink for the news. He had run nearly to Ponkert. So he babbled out his story to any who would listen, and they were many, but I fear he did not drink. I know Ponkert men! Then, when everyone in town had gone to kill the jeweler, the beggar came to me.

"They had over an hour's start, but my horse was fast and my spurs were sharp. I reached him just in time to save him from death by the spear of a tanner. I struck the tanner over the head with my sword, this very sword that you see here, but not to kill him, only to stun. Still, I struck too hard and addled his wits, so that he has been an idiot ever since. You have seen him often. He helps the blacksmith with his work—the heavy work that takes no skill. We took the jeweler to the barracks, and he told us his tale.

"Ivga, we were hardened soldiers, used to battle, murder and sudden death, crimes and horrors of all descriptions, but some among us were sickened as he told us the things that had been done to him and the sights he had seen. And the pity of it was that it had not been voluntary—he had

76

sold his soul, but under the compulsion of a black fiend, a monster that he called the master, but whom we knew could be none but the Arch-enemy in person.

"There was not a man of us with dry eyes when he told, in his dreary voice, of the manner in which this master had forced him to kill his wife and carry his baby girl out for the pack; all because he had tried to escape from the one who owned him body and soul.

"He asked for our help, and we gave it. We fought Satan and lived—most of us. And, although we killed all the pack in a trap, the master escaped and still lives—somewhere. Of course we could not kill him. He was no man to be killed.

"So we brought back the jeweler and imprisoned him in a dungeon until he recovered from wounds that he had suffered in the fight. In the meantime, I sent a report to the king.

"The royal command returned that we should end the existence of the werewolves of Ponkert by making an example of the one that remained; that his hide should be tanned, and upon it written the story of his fall to warn any who might learn of it that the master was to be shunned.

"Then came word, as he lay in prison, that his baby was not dead. It had been rescued by a hunter in the forest. Secretly, I told him, for, although there were orders that he should not know, I pitied him. He asked my promise that I would always fill a father's place in her life. I gave my oath, the oath of a Helgar which has never been broken. Later, in his confession, I read that he wished he had known me earlier so that we might have been friends. It would have been well for both of us. He was a brave spirit, for there was a smile on his lips and a jaunty tilt to his hat, as he went to the gallows.

"His name was Wladislaw Brenryk, and I have kept my promise to him. You are his daughter, a fact that no one has ever dared to tell you, for fear of me!

"Your father's skin was made into a book, bound in

leather, and hung from the gallows for a time. Then it was removed to the church, where it now is."

The stars told that midnight was near, when, from the streets, a girl entered Ponkert's church. Beneath it were hewn many cells in the living rock, and into one of these she came from out a labyrinth of underground passages. The light of the candle she bore showed that the mark of tears was on her pale cheecks, and her face was set in old lines. By Dmitri's directions she had found the correct room, although she had never been beneath the church before, and, alone, she entered unobserved.

Every man and woman in Ponkert knew the whereabouts of that cell, and the horror it contained. All who could read the book of human hide—and they were few—had done so, but no one was unfamiliar with the story written in it. Yet, so powerful is dread that while Dmitri Helgar walked in the streets, his ever present sword with him, no word was ever spoken where the girl might hear. Although she had heard of the werewolf pack that long ago had laid waste the country—it was the one event that Ponkert had of which to boast, people marking time from the slaughter of the pack—she had never imagined that Dmitri was not her father.

Now the living and the dead were to meet for the first time.

She advanced timidly into the dark room. There was no visible means of ventilation, but the air was dry and pure. A rough bench stood in a far corner. This, with the exception of a heavy stool, was the only article of furniture that the room contained. Upon the bench lay a long taper and materials for its lighting. Beside them, out of any possible reach of moisture or decay, the book lay, covered by a linen cloth.

She lit the tape and fixed it in its socket on the wall. Then, reverently, she lifted away the cloth and touched the book with loving fingers.

All that remained on earth of the father she had never known, lay before her between two, thick leather covers. The book was chained to a staple deep sunk in the wall.

Softly her white fingers stroked the pages of human parchment, and a sob caught in her throat. Her whole being called out for her unknown parents, for some affection in her love-starved existence. Only those who have never known the love of a mother can realize the value of it.

Now all the suppressed longing of her life came rushing upon her, and she cried aloud in the stillness. "Oh, father! Mother! If I could only see you once! I am so lonely and so afraid. Can't you help your little girl?"

There was no sign nor answer in the cell. The taper burned evenly as before. She lifted the cover and began to read. From the pages it seemed that her father was speaking, as though the account had been written for her alone. To his daughter, the Werewolf of Ponkert told his tragic story across the years. As she read how he had met the master and was enslaved; of his mental agony as he tried to break loose from his miserable bondage; of his final success, she began to hate the master with a deep, abiding hate.

It was he who had broken three lives along with countless others. It was he who had escaped unhurt when his poor victims had been killed in the ruined castle. It was he who even now roamed somewhere, scheming to accomplish more evil. To what purpose?

None of those he injured had harmed him, yet like a fiend he passed from one crime to another. Behind him were broken hearts and blasted lives. A bitter anger against him seized the girl. Anger turned to wonder, for, in the silent room, something else was moving!

A sweet peace drowned her black wrath, and though nothing was visible, a still small voice murmured. Not with the gross ear of flesh was the sound intercepted, but with the inner sense that yearned so desperately for love.

And the voice said, "Hate him not, my darling. He has suffered more than we."

CHAPTER III

She stared vainly around the chamber.

"Who spoke?" she said, her voice rasping loud and harsh in the quiet room.

The contrast told her instantly that it was no mortal who was present. The calm and beautiful tones flowed placidly on. One felt that the stranger was beyond human passions, a disinterested spectator of the earthly struggle.

"Hate soils the mind, Ivga. Hate no one. Pity him rather. That would hurt him more, if he knew. His proud spirit can not bear to be pitied. The master likes to rule over all and denies that he is unhappy, but we who know his sorrow pity him, though we can never forgive.

"Bitter times are coming, little daughter. We cannot help you, but we are watching near you always. In your darkest hour, do what you believe is right, and you will be happy."

The voice faded and died away. On her forehead Ivga felt a light touch, and a dainty perfume drifted by. For a second the girl felt that she was being watched by many benignant eyes; then an ineffable sense of peace and security soothed her trouble, and her unseen observers had gone.

In the chamber, far beneath the ground and secure from any drafts, the lighted taper flickered. Again that sweet fragrance permeated the atmosphere in elusive wisps. Just once she thought she heard the faint rustle of a woman's skirts, then nothing.

She stared about the chamber. Already, doubt was invading her mind. Yet the tape had not done with trembling, and the aroma still lingered.

"Oh, mother! My mother!" she whispered. "I have heard you. I have! But I wish I could have seen you. I would have loved you so much!"

She closed the book and replaced the cloth over it. Then, relighting her candle, she blew out the taper flame and left the cell. By the time she came from the church, it was well past midnight, and a brave wind rumpled her hair about her face as she stepped out upon the street.

There is something in the feel of the rushing air which blows away the unhealthy miasmas from the brain, so that Ivga had not walked far before she felt more at ease. Her steps quickened, as though she journeyed toward a meeting, yet she was scarcely aware of the direction in which she was traveling. Dimly conscious that she was within the forest, she realized that she had passed her home and turned back.

As she did so, there came a sweet music of plucked strings far away, and then a clear voice singing in the distance, and coming up the forest path from the road she had left.

The words were simple; the pathetic song of an elf to his fairy sweetheart who had deserted him for a mortal lover. The air was familiar to her, but the voice was new. Upon a stone by the side of the path, she sat and drew a leafy bough down about her. Waiting there, she was hidden and could listen to the strange voice and perhaps see who the singer was that sang in the night. The song came nearer. . . .

It is necessary to go back a little. After the caravan had made camp and food had been properly disposed of, young Gunnar and a companion returned to the village to see the new sights. He looked for the girl as they passed the cottage, but she was nowhere to be seen, and the two went on.

In Ponkert, after hours of music, wine and dance, where Hugo made pleasure for the villagers with his bandura by playing and ballads of far times and places, his companion left the young singer. Later, Hugo also quitted the tavern and commenced back to camp.

As he walked, his pockets chinked pleasantly, for Hugo's songs were not free. Somewhat stimulated by the load of coin and inward excitement he unslung the bandura from his back and swept his fingers across the strings. Taking a shorter way through the forest than the road would prove, he walked among the trees, singing as he moved.

Dancing down a beam of light
  There came a dainty fairy sprite.
Too well she loves a mortal
  Though he is in rags bedight.

When wandering over hill or plain,
  Laughing rill or stormy main,
She's guarding him from every woe;
  His sorrow is her pain.

His mortal eyes are blind to thee;
  This glorious love he cannot see.
How canst thou vainly love him so
  And never glance at me?

Abruptly the song was cut short. Something darker than the shadows had moved in the gloom beneath a low branched tree. Quick as thought itself, the boy hurled him-

83

self at the prowler, for the times were hard. Men did not skulk for any good purpose by the side of the road, watching passerbys at night, and attack was ever the best mode of defense.

The two bodies struck together, and the spy was overthrown by the blow, falling face down in a patch of moonlight, lying there very quietly.

The dagger was ready in the young man's hand as he bent over the prostrate figure and gripped it roughly by the shoulder. A second later, his fingers loosened on the blade, and it dropped to the sod. He sprang to his feet as though his hand had been bitten, whipped off his plumed, red cap and stood there, face fiery with shame and embarrassment, stammering idiotic apologies to the crumpled girl who lay still, face hidden in her arms.

Inanity after inanity stuttered forth in French, Hungarian, and Romany dialects, and receiving no answer, he began to back away, forgetting his dagger. Before he had taken two steps, his heel caught in a root and flung him solidly to the earth.

The breath whooped out of him in an explosive grunt.

Startled silence was broken by a strange sound from the girl. He saw that her shoulders quivered, and then the sound was repeated—a delighted, half-defiant, half-frightened giggle.

He was beside her on his knees at once. At least, judging by her voice and contours, she was not very old. Nor did she seem to be angry.

"Are you laughing at me?" he whispered. "Let me see your face. Please! I am sorry I struck you. I thought you were a robber. Please!" And gentle, questing fingers found her chin and turned her head.

Recognition was instant and mutual. Both smiled as each recognized the other, for although they had met and parted in a few minutes without a word between them, to each had come something that bound them irresistably together. That rare, fine emotion was theirs which only a few ever know, a tender joy in each other's presence that when one is gone makes of life an empty and useless thing for the other left alone. And now, while they gazed upon each other once again, firmer grew the bonds of love, and it seemed that they were not late acquaintances, but had been friends and lovers.

"I crave your pardon," said the boy. "I wanted so much to see you again, and now I have hurt you. I grieve!"

"You wished to see me?" amazedly questioned the girl, and he smiled in return. He had known before she spoke that her voice would be sweet, and now the very accent seemed dearly familiar.

"Me?" said Ivga. "You do not know who I am!"

"I know. Mirko, the chief, has told me of you. I believe you have been unjustly persecuted, and I would like to be your friend, if I may."

"I have no friends," she answered, now sitting up cross legged, small hands on her knees, eyeing him wide eyed and solemn. "Never has anyone wanted to be my friend but Dmitri."

Hugo felt a hot tide of jealousy surge through him— jealousy that anyone but him should be in the heart of this strange girl—jealousy that quickly passed as she continued. "But Dmitri is old and you are young like me. I have never played with anyone who was not afraid of me."

"I am not afraid of you," stoutly asserted the boy.

"No, I do not think you are. And I am glad we can be friends. I like you; do you like me?" she asked, with the charming simplicity of a little child.

"Very much," was the ardent reply.

"Then my name is Ivga—Brenryk." She hesitated over the last, unfamiliar name. "And yours?"

"I am Hugo Gunnar, late of France, and now a gipsy wanderer."

85

"You do not look like a gipsy, though I saw you with them at dusk, so big on your horse. Do you lead your band?"

Gunnar wondered just how much she knew, decided not to risk it, and modestly admitted that he didn't exactly command the troop, but left the vague idea that his was the guiding mind. The girl was properly impressed and said so.

So, in the age old way, two had met and were on the way toward love and life together.

From that meeting, apparently so casual, innocent and ordinary, events were to spring that would stay the course of progress for many years in Europe, deal civilization itself a mighty blow from which it is even yet recovering. Mighty forces were busy that night, unseen and undreamed of by the chatting couple, and it is not too much to believe that the entire meeting had been foreseen and arranged.

But the two were conscious of none but themselves. For them the world was now a pleasant place, and for Ivga, this was the first happiness since she was old enough to know that she was hated.

So the night wore on. The stars paled in the east, and still they talked, until reluctantly the girl felt that she must return.

"Come," she said. "Walk with me through the wood. I will go home now."

Hand in hand, like children, they strolled beneath the shadowing trees toward the Helgar cottage, and the way was all too short for both. They stopped at the door, but Hugo did not release her hand.

"Tomorrow, I shall see you?" It was more a statement than a question that he whispered.

"Yes, tomorrow," she breathed—hesitated—then with a flash of daring, she said, "would it were morning now!"

Desire flamed up in his eyes, and he took a step toward her. Frightened at her audacity, she had already snatched her fingers from his warm clasp and slipped through the door.

As she entered, he caught her shoulder, and his arms went about her to hold her close, a prisoner there, all woman now, and yearning for his touch. Her lips sought his and clung for a moment. Then her hands fluttered against his chest like prisoned birds, and she pushed him away.

Sobbingly, "We must not. I am the Werewolf's daughter. Please go away."

"I love you," he cried. "I would love you no matter what you were!" and he seized her fiercely again.

"You hurt me!" she wailed, softly. "Please let me go."

The blood of many nobles told. His arms went limp. The hand upon her shoulders slipped down her arm in a long caress and touched her fingers. Slowly he bowed his head as one might to some lovely, imperious princess, kissed her small palm, and closed her fingers over it.

"Keep this for me—until tomorrow," he murmured. "I am sorry. I love you. Good night."

"Tomorrow," she echoed in just the ghost of a whisper, and the door closed.

A short time he stood in the pebbled path, thoughtfully gazing at the unresponsive door. Then he went back along the road.

Somewhere he had mislaid his dagger. Was his heart also mislaid beyond the finding? He did not know.

CHAPTER IV

They had spoken of tomorrow, but the word should have been today to be truthful. As Hugo walked into camp, little birds were singing in that half light which heralds morning. He lay down in his usual cart with his clothes on, for he knew the call would soon come for arising. Before he was near sleep, a harsh peal brayed out from the cook's wagon, and soon that dignitary appeared in the open, a cow's horn in hand. Upon this he blew a second blast, and a general stir of rising and sleepy grunts of protest were heard from the covered carts.

Hugo slipped from his bed, and, being already dressed, was one of the first to help at kindling fire. Now a bustle of yapping dogs told of breakfast, and things began to appear more cheery to tired men as they had something to kick at and curse. Breakfast vanished with speed and in large quantities, and the business of the day began.

This was the first morning of the three days in Ponkert, and there was much work to do. The camp was not yet completely set in order, and there was tugging and hauling of carts into positions better than the hurried selections of the night before. Driven by the gruff orders of Mirko, men scurried about, setting up a little platform at one end of the open ground. Upon this stage, with the forest for a back drop and the sky for a canopy, entertainment would be presented for the villagers. At the other end, near the road, a heap of rock arose as if by magic and was quickly formed into a rude but serviceable forge. A portable smithy was a necessity to such a troop, and to it, after the few horses that had cast shoes had been shod again, Hugo repaired in a moment's leisure. In his hand, he bore an odd weapon. In length, it was all of four feet. It might have been termed a sword, except that it had neither edge nor point. It was nothing more than a rod of steel, fixed into a basket sword-hilt, as thick as a man's thumb where it joined the hilt, and oval rather than round. It tapered rapidly toward the tip, where it was, perhaps, a quarter of an inch in thickness and the same in breadth.

This blunt tip, Hugo thrust into the coals, and plying the bellows, he soon had a leaping flame. When the steel had taken the desired color, he drew it out. With a small hammer, he commenced to draw out the tip to a point of exceeding fineness. He was engaged upon this work when he heard a voice behind. Ivga stood there.

Dropping the hammer, he snatched off his cap and made a low salutation.

"A wondrous morning," he smiled. "I trust your majesty slept well?"

"Divinely," she returned in the same joking spirit. "But not long."

"I warrant," said the boy. "Would you like to walk about the camp?"

So, by his side, Ivga saw the little stage where tumblers were at practice, visited a blind harper who played a quaint air of the southland, and was introduced to an old woman whom the youth called Clauda, who crossed herself furtively as the girl turned her head away to watch a half-tamed wolf fighting with a dog from the town. For, by this time, a sprinkling of villagers were mingling with the gipsies, and certain silver pieces were already in different pouches than they were at daybreak.

Clauda, now that she was not noticed, skulked into a tent, lifted the back flap, and by a roundabout way, keeping out of sight of the girl, gained her own tent and did not return. None knew better than old Clauda the danger of being old and lean and odd of face. Many an old woman had crackled at a stake on no better proof of witchery, and to be seen with such a suspicious one as this girl when townsmen were about savored to Clauda most strongly of suicide. She was not seen about the grounds until the girl had gone.

The departure was somewhat hastened by a crowd of children, who, increasing in numbers and boldness, followed the two as they moved from one curious scene to another. At last they became noisy and virulent, and Hugo turned upon them, jaw outthrust and eyes blazing.

"What's odd with you?" he scowled. "Did you never see me before? Can I not walk with a lady without a company at my heels?"

It was a town boy that answered from a mind biased by the prejudices of his elders.

"You I know not, nor care to. But the lady"—an unpleasant accent on the word—"that you have with you, we know well. And a most sickening smell of sulfur clings to her!"

Hugo caught him a clout with a hard fist that sent him reeling, but the girl prevented the blow from being followed by another. White faced, she drew him away.

"I am sorry. I have brought trouble to you," she said, when they were again alone. "I should not have come." And she walked along with her gaze upon the road.

"Do not mind them, Ivga," he comforted. "It was but

children's talk. They know no better."

"Not all," she replied, sorrowfully. "They all hate me here. Where did he learn that? From what others say about me, who would love them all. It was only a word, but a spark shows the direction of a wind, and little words like that will light a flame against me soon."

"Is it as bad as that?" the youth asked.

"Dmitri has advised me not to leave his sight any more," was the indirect answer.

"And you disobeyed to see me!" Hugo exclaimed joyfully.

Ivga laughed a little. "How I do talk on such a lovely day! Let us be happy and save this for some other time. Let us go to the woods, and I will show you Ponkert from the old haunted castle on the hill."

"But I must work," Hugo protested, more than willing for a holiday, but wondering what Mirko would think of his delinquency.

"Love you your task then?" she pouted. "Why, go you to it, if you must." And she turned toward the forest path.

"Wait!" he cried. "I will come. Let me get my sword." He ran back to the forge and recovered the uncompleted weapon.

She was waiting in the forest when he came. They walked through the woods, and, she teased him about his weapon. This toy was no sword for a man to carry; nay, it was no sword at all, but only a knitting needle that she could use herself. Now, her father had a sword that was worth seeing. Seeing Hugo's glum look, she became penitent and was forgiven, but first exacted a promise that he would come on the morrow to see her foster father's sword. He, in return, offered to bring Clauda to tell the fortunes of both the girl and Dmitri.

At last they came to the old ruined castle upon the hill overlooking the river, forest, Ponkert, and the plain. Here, resting beneath the very crumbling wall which once the master had leaped to safety, the youth observed another mountain far away near the river which almost encircled Ponkert, but on the other side of the village. The top of this peak was divided in two, as though split down part way with a giant's axe. Curious, he asked its name.

"It has no name," replied Ivga. "I call it my mountain, for I am there much. On the side near the river, father and I have a little boat where we go to fish and play. Or we did, long ago." She fell silent, thinking of far off happy days when Dmitri's legs were strong.

"It must be hard to climb," he said idly, not dreaming of the conditions that would soon cause him to know just how hard it was to gain the summit.

"It is," said Ivga, "very hard. No one goes there but me. I can be all alone up there and forget how people hate me and be happy with the wind. And when I am all alone, so high, I feel closer to heaven, mother, and my father too. They are happy because they are dead and have each other. They loved and were not long apart after mother died. What father did was not his fault. He was made into a werewolf; he did not seek it, as many have. Because of that, they hate me."

"I do not hate you, Ivga," said Hugo, and took her hand. "Have you forgotten last night and what we said this morning?"

The curls shook vigorously. "No, but you were wrong. You did not know I was so bad. You said you—loved me." She looked down at the distant village. "They will hurt you some way if you stay here. You must go away when the band goes. You will find someone else, better than I am"—the words caught in her throat, but she went on bravely with a steady voice—"someone not cursed. And I hope you will be very happy with her."

There were tears in her dark eyes now, but her voice did not tremble. "So it is a pretty dream, but it must die.

No one can ever love me. Never!" The brown head sank low. "I am the Werewolf's daughter, shunned, hated, and feared by all, cursed at birth and despised by even the children. There is not, nor can there be, any love or rest for me in all this ugly world," she said bitterly, and drew her hand away.

"Peace," he whispered, and laid his fingers across her sullen lips. "I love you, and shall love you always."

"How can you be so sure?" she breathed.

He bent his head, and seeing the look in her eyes, kissed her cheek; then, gently daring, found her lips with his—and was not denied.

She lay quiescent in his strong embrace, and presently her arms went about his neck and drew him closer. Held captive, a willing prisoner, he felt as though his wandering was at an end, and he was come home at last.

She moved away and looked at him, studying his earnest face.

"Hugo, what are we to do? Will you take me with you when you go?"

"I could not," he said, frightened at the thought. "You would not be safe with us. Anything might happen. No, I will stay here with you."

"That I will not have you do. It is more dangerous here for you than it would be for me to go, but—" she paused.

"What is it?"

"Dmitri; I cannot go. He would be all alone."

The youth started to speak, but she smiled. "Never mind. We will forget it and be happy now while we can. Tell me a story, Hugo. Now—you are from France, you say. Is it far away?"

"Very, very far. Many days' journey, even for horses."

"I have heard tales of France, but I have never seen it," said the girl, wistfully, as she sat gazing across the valley, hands locked about her knees. "Tell me, is it a lovely land?"

Hugo, remembering his home, knew it to be beautiful, and being far away, memories portrayed it still more pleasantly than he had known it. From that picture, he described his home and country, finishing: "In France the flowers are lovelier and more fragrant than here; the birds carol sweeter because they are French. Why, even the sun shines brighter over Blois than Ponkert! And the blue of the sky! Oh, Ivga, you can not imagine how lovely it all is. I think the floor of heaven must hang very low over Blois!"

"Well," decided the girl in a judicious tone, "it is nice up here, too, sometimes. And now for the story. I must have a story."

Hugo grinned. "Must? Listen then and I will tell a story of my family, long ago. And then you will know why I am not afraid of a werewolf's little daughter.

"It is told of our house, that very long ago there was a count who lived under a dreadful spell, being at certain changes of the moon sorely afflicted by a transformation of his body into that of a wolf.

"At such times, he would roam the forests after hiding his clothes in a sure place known only to himself. It was part of the witchery that without his clothes he might never resume his shape.

Now the count's wife was evilly disposed toward him, yearning greatly toward a young soldier of the castle guard. With diligent and tormenting questions, she discovered his secret and watched for an opportunity.

"When he wandered again, she followed at a distance, stole his garments from their concealment, and fled to the castle. After a decent time, she gave out that the count was dead. But his magic garb she laid away."

"Why didn't she burn them?" the girl inquired logically.

"I don't know," Hugo confessed. "It didn't seem very wise of her, but she did keep them.

"The count roamed the country for long, after he knew

94

he could not become a man again, and his heart was full of wrath against his faithless lady. He went hungry often when he might have eaten, for he would not slay the innocent and helpless, but preyed only on real wolves and dangerous animals of the forests. He became gaunt with famine, and his body scarred with battles, so that one day when the nobles were hunting, and the dogs cried behind him, he could not outrun them.

"He burst through the pack and laid hold with his teeth upon the stirrup of the king, who was among the hunters and whom he had known in his former life."

"O-oh!" gasped Ivga. "Did they kill him?"

"Not at all," Hugo answered. "They were going to do so, but the gracious king saw there were tears in the wolf's eyes, and that he fawned piteously upon those who came to spear him, rubbing against their legs like a cat. The king, sensing sorcery, commanded that the werewolf should be given quarters in the palace until such time as he should regain his former shape, and that he should be called 'Gunnar.'

"While he dwelt among them, many tried their skill at breaking the spell, but to no avail. One day, a great ball was held at the palace. Nobles from all the country were present, and in their number came the heartless lady, now wived to her guilty lover. While they danced in gay ignorance, Gunnar rose from where he had lain couched before the throne as a trusted pet, and with a silent bound flung himself upon the defilers of his honor. Her paramour he slew, but contented himself with one snap at his false lady, which left her noseless to her death.

"Then great excitement arose. Many claimed that the attack was cruel and unjust, and these clamored for the wolf's death. The wise king, however, mistrusting the countess, caused her to be so treated that she confessed the truth and located the magic garments for the werewolf. No sooner had he donned them than he became the count and fell at the king's feet, swearing fealty anew to his just rule. From that time, he took the name of Gunnar in gratefulness to the king. His former marriage was annulled, and he married again, more happily than before. And, although he was always subject to the enchantment at moon change, he ever found his garments where he had placed them, and no hunters were allowed to enter the woods he ranged.

"So you see, little witch, that even if your father was a werewolf, one of my kin was also. Perhaps I might be one too; who knows? Aren't you afraid of me?" He smiled into her face as she looked up at him.

"Not if you love me as much as I do you," she replied demurely, with a twinkle in her eyes.

"Love you, Ivga? I worship you; but take care! Don't tease me too much, because you look sweet enough to eat, and I might begin any time. Thus!" And he caught her hands in his and began kissing each fingertip in turn, while she touched her lips softly to his thick, black hair.

Feeling the gentle pressure, he lifted his head quickly, and their lips met. Then a teasing mood seized him. He cried, "Be careful! Now I am a werewolf. I have you, little one! Shall I bite off your nose?"

"If you can catch me!" she laughed as she slipped deftly from his eager arms and ran away toward the river. Her skirts fluttered about her nimble limbs, and, with flushed and happy face, she was a picture of happiness. It is good to love and to be loved for the first time when one has been very lonely. And now believing that Hugo had a dark blot upon his ancestry as well, she did not feel so terribly isolated and alone in her misery. Nor did she ever know that he had lied to her with that exact object in his mind at the time, relating an old legend for her benefit as history and truth.

Shouting hoarsely, in mock rage, he followed, and by the river bank he caught her fast in his arms and held her close.

"Now you are mine," he panted, "and I shall not let you go. You are mine for always, for I love you.

"We will go away from here," he murmured. "We will go back to my father in Blois, who is very rich, and you will be his dear daughter and my love."

"But Dmitri? I can't go without him!" she said in alarm. "I can't leave him while he lives."

"We'll take him, too," the boy promised largely. "Our castle is big. There is room enough for all of us."

And they sealed the bargain with a kiss.

The sun hung low when they left the river bank and wandered back toward home, talking together in low tones, and planning far ahead. Yet, while they chatted, each happily conscious of the other's adoration, events were marching to a dreadful conclusion in Ponkert.

The morning before, a woodchopper had gone to his work in the Old Forest. Two days had all but passed, and he had not returned. At that moment, a small band of men were in the forest, searching patiently in the evening gloom.

As the sun went down, two men trudged home from their work in Ponkert. Tired, they sometimes stopped to rest. Passing the house of Helgar, they noticed that the door was open, and glanced within. The old man lay sleeping in his chair, covered with a robe.

The day had been long for him without Ivga. He had worried, but she had said that she might be gone some while. The river was low, and many of the fish had died, so that the fishing that she purposed to do might not be quickly done. And now he slept and dreamed of Ivga.

One of the workmen nudged his fellow. It was the former tanner, now crazed—on one subject worse than the rest: revenge for the blow which had made him so.

"See!" he muttered to his companion, an evil-browed lout. "He is alone. Is now the time?"

The blacksmith frowned. Always it was necessary to

watch his mad helper lest he do himself or others a mischief.

"Not yet," he answered. "Come away. Some other time; not now."

The idiot grinned vacuously and resisted the other's restraining clutch, making as though to open the gate, while he loosened the knife by his side.

"He struck me once," he growled, as he struggled to be free.

The other man gripped him fiercely. "You cursed fool; now is not the time! The soldiers would be about our ears like bees. Some day they will all be gone. Wait!"

"I have waited fifteen years," he grumbled. "You always say that!" He allowed himself to be urged down the road.

"He struck me once!" the former tanner repeated, and turned for a last look.

Two persons were coming up from the village, walking slowly. He stopped short, holding back the smith.

"Look! It is the witch," he muttered. "She has trapped a gipsy. He will die within the week!"

"Nay!" denied the smith, as he saw who walked beside the girl. "I saw them this morning walking together, and he went willingly. 'Tis no beguilement of hers."

"He went willingly? Then he is a sorcerer too! Are you mad as these fools say I am? Would he go with her, knowing what she is, were he not as bad or worse? He is another menace to the town, and they should both be burned."

The smith blinked stupidly at the idea. He was not quick of wit, and the thought seemed good to him.

"You are right, Wesoskas," he unwillingly agreed, revolving within his dull brain plans by which he might tell others on the morrow of the wondrous idea and by naming the boy as a sorcerer gain fame and credit for being a man of keen insight among the village folk.

They moved along, talking, and behind them came the girl and Hugo, having no eyes for anything but each other. Neither suspected how the threads of destiny were being wound together into a cord that might mean death for all.

CHAPTER V

Women talked in little groups the next morning, and there was a general air of suspense and expectancy in Ponkért for the most of the day. It began at sunrise with a story told by one of those who had been at the gipsy camp, and, in the repeating, the tale grew huge and dangerous.

As told by a woman in a group by the village well, it ran something like this: "You have not heard the evil that befell my little Millo? Yesterday he said something to the witch when she was at the gipsy camp, and she told a great brute of a gipsy that was with her to kill him. The beast knocked my poor boy down and trampled on him, but he crawled away. Then she cursed him—and see! When he was coming home, he climbed a tree to swing on the branches, and a branch broke. His leg is broken now. May her bones be crumbled in fire or rot away while she lives!"

"Aye," chimed in another. "Remember how my lad was killed. Just for striking her with a stone, it was, in child-ish fun. Was he not missing only a month later, and found buried in the sand pit where she had caused the bank to slide upon him?

"Remember the widow of Capelok's pigs? How they sickened and died after she was found watching them one day and the old woman drove her away?"

"And the blinding of young Switte only last season? Recall the day he was led out of the wood, half mad, with his eyes blown out, when his gun exploded! Did he not say that the witch had punished him for staring at her over long?"

So the tales flew, each natural calamity discussed only from one point of view, and all revolving around a single hub—the suspected witch.

Was the summer dry, so that the crops were poor and the river low? The witch was to blame!

Did sheep die from an odd sickness that year? Ivga again! And ever through the talk that day ran two recurring motifs—the sending of a curse on Millo the day before, as he had lyingly claimed to his mother, and the yet unsolved mystery of the missing woodchopper now in his third day of absence.

The searchers had straggled in late the night before, their hunt to no purpose, and now they were gone again. They searched the woods and hills systematically, with slow, patient care, where before they had been more hurried and less thorough. For now all knew he must be dead.

And through the village a suspicion grew hourly more defined, though no one knew who first had uttered it, that the manner of his passing had not been a natural one. People longed with a dreadful, sadistic desire that the thing they suspected would prove true.

What was it that had killed the missing man?

Not a hint of this unrest came to the cottage beside the road, for no one tarried that passed that way. Hugo had heard rumors early in the day when he brought Clauda, the future reader, to visit the girl, but he said nothing to alarm her.

Clauda was less considerate. She had had no desire to come, and only Hugo's insistence that she oblige him, and his positive belief that she would not be seen had brought her there. Once there, she dispatched her business in haste, and left with no wish to linger.

From an inkhorn she poured a black pool into Dmitri's palm and peered into it, her small, sunken eyes restlessly seeking for knowledge. Dmitri, unbelieving and skeptical, asked if she could see him walking in that pool of ink.

"Yes," said old Clauda. "Once more you will walk, once more you shall fight, but from that fight you come back never. No feat of arms shall slay you, but I see you dying among a heap of slain. Rocky walls on each side reach high. It is dark. I can see no more."

"If no trick of battle causes my end," said Dmitri, "who then shall kill me? Can you see? Look again."

"His face I cannot see. The night is heavy on the battle-field, but this I know. A dead man shall slay thee."

"You speak in riddles, Clauda," said Hugo, vexed by such an unhappy introduction to Ivga's guardian, and fearing lest this might prove a poor beginning for all his great plans.

"You brought me here. I did not wish to come. I have told the truth!"

"Do not be angry, Clauda," said the youth, coaxingly. "A nice reading now for Ivga, please. What is her future to be?"

"Pour the ink. I will not touch her hand, Pour the ink youself."

Hugo filled the girl's hand with the fluid, and the old crone bent over the pool with mingled dread and curiosity. A long time she looked, and as they watched, her face grew white and strained. At last she looked up.

"I can see nothing," Clauda said evenly. "I will not look again. Come back with me, Hugo. There is danger here."

"After a little time, mother, after a little." The boy

laughed away his own disturbed thoughts.

"Woe and sorrow rest upon this house!" wailed the crone, and then returned to camp.

After she had gone, Ivga showed him Gate-Opener, and Dmitri told him all that he knew about it. Together, they disposed of his worry over the reading of the prophetess and made him feel more easy and at home.

Not even the grandfather of Dmitri knew much of Gate-Opener's past, save that its age was great. Its very appearance spoke of antiquity to those who knew swords well. Hugo's cheek flushed as he gazed upon it and compared it to that other almost legendary sword, Durandal, which it so much resembled.

"From similar times they came," thought the boy. "Perchance it may have swung and flickered icily upon some battlefield where thirsty Durandal was also drinking deep from the cup of a shattered skull."

So, dreaming of mightier days, he patted the hilt of the keen and ponderous brand.

When Hugo had quite finished with admiring the enormous broadsword, Ivga commanded with a delightfully imperious air of ownership that the boy show his own tiny weapon. Reluctantly, he drew his rapier and laid it across the old man's knees. Although four feet long, beside Gate-Opener it was as insignificant as a dagger.

Dmitri's voice was grave, but about his lips there lurked the faintest suspicion of a smile, while Ivga did not trouble to hide her amusement at this ridiculous comparison.

"What might be the use of this toy?" asked Dmitri, his pleasant voice taking some of the sting from the words.

"Sire," replied the boy, bowing to hide the quick flush of resentment, "In the right hands, it is capable of making widows."

"Ah?" queried Dmitri. "And has it been used for that purpose?"

"Not as yet, sire, for it is but lately finished. The point

103

I made this morning."

"Then how can you be so certain of its worth?"

"Its value has been proved in battle," replied Hugo proudly. "My father was the first to fight with this type of sword, and it began thus:

"When my father was a very young man, our castle was besieged by an enemy who at one time entered the walls and almost conquered us. The fighting was hand to hand, and all who could bear arms fought beside our men-at-arms and peasants. My father chanced to have his sword broken in his hand and was beaten to his knees by the man who fought against him. As the man swung up his sword to cleave my father in two, father's hand fell upon a fragment of spear, and leaning forward beneath the descending blade, he ran the soldier through.

"When the battle was over and we had won, father, being of an ingenious turn of mind, bethought himself of a new weapon, in shape a sword, but to be used in an unusual way. It should remain secret and thus carry surprise with it. It should be edgeless, therefore round, and amazing sharp in point like a cook's spit. It should be light in weight, the easier to parry with, and possess a good grip for the hand. Here you see it."

Dmitri examined the primitive rapier critically.

"It has a wicked look, yet it is made for boys, not men to play with. Old Gate-Opener here," and he slapped the hilt of the broadsword affectionately, "would make six of this—this—" he hesitated.

"Knitting needle!" supplied Ivga, laughing.

"To every man his weapon," smiled the youth, but the smile was only with his lips. "Would you see how one may play with it?"

Without waiting for an answer, he snatched his rapier from the old man's lap and sheathed it, then walked to the fireplace and selected a billet of wood nearly four inches thick. Standing near the wall, he tossed the stick into the

104

air. Before it had begun to fall, he whipped out his sword more quickly than the eye could see the motion. Dmitri and Ivga heard a thud, and the boy stepped back empty handed. Against the wall of the room the rapier trembled, driven through the stick, which it had pinned to the wall.

"Now," said Hugo, quizzically, "if that had been a man?"

Dmitri did not show the surprise he felt. "Is the steel as strong as your wrist?" he asked.

"Nearly!" Hugo grinned. "See!"

Seizing the hilt, he tore the rapier from the wall and set his foot upon the stick, then pressing sideways, bent the slender blade into an arc, after which he pulled it from the stick and returned it to the old man for examination. The point was apparently as needle sharp as before.

"My father taught me many things with such toys, and my brothers and I have practiced daily with them since we were strong enough to lift one. Ours is the only family which knows their value."

Dmitri, having learned all that he wished, changed the subject abruptly.

"You spoke of 'our castle'," he said, bluntly. "Does that mean that you are a noble in your own land?"

"The name of Gunnar is famous in France. I am a Gunnar!"

"Then how come it that you trail with gipsies?"

"I was headstrong and the youngest son," answered Hugo, soberly. "Father and I quarreled. So I am here. Is it an answer?"

"It is enough," replied Dmitri. "Ivga, will you bring us wine?"

In this way, the two who each in his way loved the friendless girl, looked upon each other and were satisfied. Each found the other a man to whom his heart warmed. So they met and parted, never to meet again, for Hugo did not enter the cottage that evening after he and Ivga had walked together along the river bank and planned and

105

planned—very far ahead that afternoon, meaning to take Dmitri with them when the caravan left.

But in after years, Hugo remembered that day and Dmitri's simple, kindly smile, so loving when he spoke to Ivga, and often wondered how the three of them could have been so blind to the shadow that all the day was gathering closer about them.

In the streets the women talked and waited. In the forest men searched, hoping, yet fearing to find what they were certain would be found.

And that for which they sought lay hidden by brush beside a fallen oak, in territory which had been gone over several times. So securely was it laid away, that only those who had cunningly hid it there knew its hiding place— only those, and now and then an inquiring fly that buzzed down hungry, and arose later on sluggish wing, flying heavily away.

So ended the second day of the caravan's three days in Ponkert.

That night the searchers did not come home, but hunted by the light of torches, and by morning were scattered thinly through the forest. The sun was two hours high when a man, leaping over a fallen tree, fell short into the brush and, for the space of a second, lay face to face with the dead.

Then from the woods arose a cry, a vengeful whooping and halloo, that rose and sank, tossed from one to another of the searchers and carried on as, when the deer is sighted, the hounds give tongue.

From all the forest rose the cry. "Found! He is found!" And from a score of points the men converged toward the spot where the body lay, until all had come and clustered around.

He was grievously torn and mangled, scarcely to be recognized as human, but they knew by certain garments and his axe that it was the woodchopper. His wood chopped, his wandering done, his axe lay idle at last.

Still and quietly he lay, and quietly, ominously so, the group of men stood and stared at the sad ruin the forest beasts had wrought. Men that search for a definite thing twist all they see toward the supporting of their belief. Every man in the band would have sworn that it was not wolves that had killed the woodsman, though the tracks were thick and plain for all to see.

Through the crowd burst a lad, fierce and wild eyed, and crying, "Where? Where?" to the men so grimly silent. Spying the body, he fell upon it, sobbing out his grief to the cold ears, for it had been his brother. Gentle hands lifted the lad away, and pitying voices mumbled stiff and stumbling words of sympathy. But the boy would have none of pity, and with the fierce intolerance of youth he struck away the comforters.

"Oh Christ!" he sobbed. "How long do we stand the curse that lies upon this town? How long do we groan under the rule of this seed of the Fiend? Sickness, famine, and sorrow have we had; the river wanes away; the sheep die; terror stalks in the streets at night; and now this! Oh, my brother, my brother, we will avenge you soon; but how much longer do we wait?"

The men shifted on uneasy feet; neighbor looked furtively at neighbor and quickly turned his glance away. Each read the other's thought and found him willing for desperate and unholy deeds as the boy raved on.

"Owned are we by this devil-chick, this werewolf's daughter! Are we slaves or men? I say to you all that if you do not help to end this menace to our happiness and lives, I will kill this witch myself!"

From the crowd, one pressed forward; the idiot tanner.

"I will help," he chuckled. "Give me old Helgar and I will help. He struck me once!"

"I will help, too," came a second voice, as another was

107

encouraged by this example and stepped to the front.

The men chorused a willingness with only a few holding back.

"Why do we wait!" cried the boy. "Come! Did you ever see wolf tracks as large as this?" He pointed to the signs in the rich loam.

Many had indeed seen larger tracks, but so distorted at this moment were their imaginations, and the majority of opinion was so great, that those who might have spoken for the girl felt the words die in their throats, for after all, they were not quite sure.

Perhaps the tracks were those of a werewolf, although they were exactly like those of a real wolf! Then they would be making a hideous mistake in attempting to save the girl. And so against their weak judgment they joined the others in the cry for the innocent blood.

So shifting is the mood of men that before the mourners reached Ponkert, they were more rabid and vicious than the young lad who had suffered most.

Spurred on by the news he bore, a runner had gasped out the story, and, as the band entered the village, a rabble met them, already armed and waiting. Like a revolutionary mob, they filled the street from side to side as all poured on, out of Ponkert to the country road.

Ivga had just taken away Dmitri's breakfast dish when gravel crunched in the path, and the door crashed open. The room was filled with noise. A dozen hands seized her and buffeted her about as one pulled her from another, striking and bruising her cruelly.

"Please! What is it? What have I done?" stammered the girl.

So many told her at once that she did not understand a word and fell silent, giving them stare for stare. Proud, defiant, unbroken, she stood and heard Dmitri bellowing curses against them all.

Loud he lamented his crippled legs, breathing terrible

108

threats against the people if Ivga were hurt. He called for a friend, if one were there, to give him his sword that she might have a defender.

They did not wish to hurt Dmitri. They respected him still, if they had no fear of him now. Well they knew what would befall them if his soldiers should know he had been injured. To silence him, as much as for any other purpose, a man reached to the wall and flung Gate-Opener down to the floor, near by, where he could not reach it from his chair.

They commenced to drag her out, Ivga not understanding what their intentions were. Dmitri, however, heard the words: "Fire!" and "Square!", and was certain of their plans. He raved, impotently.

And, while he, noisy in his frantic wrath, shrieked damnation against them, there came to a listener in the crowd the memory of a long-unavenged wrong, which now would be satisfied as men had promised in the forest that it should be.

CHAPTER VI

The idiot tanner lurched forward through the crowd, his eyes shining with a mad, fanatical light. "He struck me once!" hissed through his yellow fangs.

Men gave him room because of his fierce aspect and the axe which he bore upon his shoulder. With a sweep of his arm, he hurled the cripple from his chair so that Dmitri lay face down, half stunned and twitching in helplessness. Close beside him lay the sword that was so impotent to aid him now.

As the maniac howled in glee and swung up his axe to strike, the girl, weak and suffering from her blows, could bear no more. Her slight form sagged limply in her captor's arms. Mercifully, she had fainted.

She did not see the hands that seized the axe in its downward sweep to halt the blow. She did not hear the men, who fearing a reprisal from the soldiers, reasoned with the maniac. While the soldiers would not interfere with the execution of a witch, they would, of a certainty, avenge the cowardly murder of their old and crippled captain.

She did not hear the ravings of the maniac, disappointed in his revenge, as he struggled to reach the cripple. The ravings continued until a promise was given that Dmitri should be given to the mercies of the former tanner, following the tortures of the girl on the morrow. It was a promise that was never intended or destined to be kept.

She did not feel herself being carried roughly out of doors, jostled and bruised in the press, while the tanner lagged far enough behind to deal one savage kick to the prostrate cripple. All these things she never knew, and to the day of her death, many years later, she believed that her foster father had met his end beneath the tanner's axe.

As the last of the raiders quitted the house, a somewhat darker shadow hovered near the cripple where he lay, hopelessly sobbing in his anger and fear for the girl. For a little space, it hovered as though watching. And then, contrary to the habits of shadows, it moved with no one near, following the path the crowd had taken.

At the village, they hastened the fainting girl to the square. They bound her fast with iron chains to the stone post, which rose above a log platform. It was an old scaffold, built for public punishment, with steps leading up from the ground. Upon it were a gallows, a wheel to the purpose of breaking bones, and the post. The latter had an iron floor about it, erected for death by fire.

Upon this structure the martyrdom of the innocent now began.

All that sultry afternoon, she hung in her chains. The fierce sun beat down upon her unprotected head, and as the day wore to a close, a throbbing began in her temples, and strange, humming noises attacked her ears. In that incredibly long afternoon, she had not known one moment's rest from the torment.

At first she answered the gibes and taunts that were flung at her by the tormentors, but it only excited them to fresh efforts.

Words failing to provide enough amusement, they began to throw other things. Mud flew, small sods, stones, offal, sticks, and once a dead cat; but her spirit was not to be broken by missiles, though her body was near to that point.

Many times she searched the howling sea of faces for Hugo, but she did not see him. There were several of the gipsy band who gave her pitying glances, but they turned away when she caught their eyes, knowing that they could not help.

At length, a group of villagers unleashed a new torment. Several men ran into the church, pried loose the staple which held the book to the underground wall, and ran back with it to the scaffold. Here they fastened it to a beam and set it swinging beside her.

The rusty chain squeaked as the book swung, and, to her delirious fancy, it seemed as though it was the voice of a man, crying beneath the torturer's knife. Father and daughter were together at last—upon the scaffold. One was dead; the other near to dying!

She bowed her head to hide the tears that formed in her sad eyes, but there were many who saw the evidence that she was hurt at last.

There was no pity in Ponkert. How they howled. More than a mile away, Dmitri heard the shout and cursed them. He knew that something new and dreadful had been devised for his loved one. But curses do little harm, and the people enjoyed themselves in their sadistic happiness until night fell.

Cruel as they were, they were careful not to kill. A greater entertainment was set for the morning, and a pile of wood and brush rose near the scaffold in readiness for the final sport.

The delay was twofold. One purpose was to torture by the night chill—to pain her bruised and stiffened muscles like sharp knives. The second was an even more refined method of torture.

The agony and suspense and waiting would make the dark hours seem like years to her. She waited for sunrise— the stake and the flaming death. Well they knew that no one could find ease or sleep while hanging in those iron chains that held the wrists.

Twilight came. The people left the square, leaving only a sentry to watch the girl that she might not call help or vanish by her diabolical arts.

As the girl hung, only partly conscious in the chains which bound her to the post, and believing Dmitri dead and Hugo to have forsaken her, she felt that all that makes life worth living had been taken away.

Suddenly, she felt something from outside calling gently, insistently, and her spirit tugged at her body, impatient to be free. Although she feared, she did not resist. Her spirit was drawn from her body like a sword from its sheath, and it hovered silently above its former shell.

As her astral self hung there, a spirit invisible to the eyes of the sentry, she seemed to have been lifted into another realm. Here there was no pain nor suffering, no hunger nor thirst, no sorrow nor delight; only a restful sense of peace that permeated her being. She longed to remain in that blissful state forever.

She felt that something held her. She looked down to see a wisp of cord connecting this new self with the body she had quitted. Quite naturally, it came to her that if the cord were broken, she would be free and the torturers that were to come in the morning would be cheated.

Timidly at first, then harder, she tugged at the cord. It gave and stretched, but would not snap. At each tug, the body in the straps quivered and twitched. At last it moaned.

The sentry started, swore at his nerves, and commenced a dreary, monotonous whistling to keep his courage.

The cord stretched thin, swaying in time with the dismal creak and whine of the heavy book which moved on its rusty chains. Soon it would part!

Then the girl felt the proximity of another, very near,

113

who radiated such an immense power that it surged in waves through her spirit like an elixir of life. Obeying an unspoken command to turn, she ceased the strain upon the cord and faced the stranger.

Instinctively, she knew that the spirit was evil. It was neither male nor female in principle, yet seemed both. Like herself it hovered, had limbs and a body, yet was not human. Its face held a sadness which coupled with an apparent confidence in its own power to overcome any obstacle; a frightful sorrow as of one who broods over lost opportunities, having made a mistake which cannot be repaired, yet knows that he is all powerful against any foe, so that the spirit's pride was arrogant and domineering.

It was a lost soul that stared into the girl's face. Still, she did not feel afraid. She had passed beyond human sensations and left them with the body, bound to the stone post. She knew this creature to be the master, but she was not afraid. As she watched, he addressed her, and his words were wondrous gentle.

"I have seen your life, your trouble, and the hate of these people for you. Long have I brooded near this village, planning to avenge myself upon your father. He betrayed me in life, although his cause was great. I have been a cruel master even to my slaves.

"Your father cheated me, even in death, dying in a manner that forbade my interference. For a time, I meant to wreak my vengeance upon you, the last of the line, trusting that he might see and be punished. You have suffered, aye, all your life you have suffered for your father's sin. Hence, it is in my mind to show you mercy. My revenge I must have, and I will! But I can wait. The years are nothing to those who are immortal.

"I give you choice this night, child of Brenryk. Become my slave and I will free you, and the score shall be evened. Also, the people of Ponkert shall suffer most deeply for that which they have done this day.

"Refuse my offer, and I shall free you still. Your lover

114

shall be yours, and all your lifetime you shall go unharmed by me. But at your death, should you leave heirs, then they shall be my fair prey. One from each generation—perhaps more—shall I take, until your line is stamped from the earth. This I promise and will fulfill! Say, girl, if from your offspring I may have one to do my will!"

"You may," said the girl, aloud, in the flat, dull tone of the hypnotic.

"It is well!" he chuckled, and then in a sly manner he sprang his trap.

"Of each generation?" was all that he said, softly and gently so that they fell upon the ears of the girl without realization of their meaning. The three words spelled sorrow, misery and terror to countless souls yet unborn, and the girl had the power, by a word, to decide the future of many.

"Yes," she said dreamily, in her bodily voice, and by the single word she slew many who were yet to be as surely as though she had laid a knife to their throats.

A look of devilish joy swept across the master's distorted face. "It is well," he said. "Your body will forget these words now. One is coming, even now, to free you."

And with these words, he disappeared from her sight forever.

CHAPTER VII

A small groan issued from the prostrate form on the floor of the cottage. The man moved his fingers slightly, as though they clenched on something. He groaned again, after which be began to mumble broken words, face in the dust.

"Oh God, help me now! Give me back my strength just for a little while. She is a pretty, little girl, and she always loved you. She is so sweet and lovable, could you let her die?"

His voice sank to a confidential murmur. "You see, I've got to go. I can't stay here while they hurt her. I promised I would always guard and keep her. Must I break my given word? It's a wicked, cruel joke to play this trick with me. I know I've been wicked in many ways, and I deserve no pity. But don't You see, it isn't for me I ask? You aren't punishing me, but the little girl. What did she ever do? I don't care what becomes of me. Take my soul and thrust it into the deepest pit of Hell, but save her! Oh, God! Give me back my strength!"

The feeble voice droned away to silence. Dmitri Helgar, mercenary Czech, captain in the Black Brigade, had finished his first prayer.

There was darkness before the fallen figure moved again. The afterglow of sunset was fading, and an early star shone.

"Strength and a sword!" exclaimed Dmitri, in a strong voice, far different from the former tone, although he had not stirred. "A sword and an arm to wield it," he said in the tones of one who sleeps yet speaks. His right arm began to raise itself upon the fingertips like a monstrous insect blindly sprawling. Like an insect, the hand crawled toward the beloved sword hilt.

The fingers missed by inches, but continued to walk as far as the arm's length would permit. Then they moved crabwise, the thumb creeping ahead, digging into the floor, and contracting, thus pulling the hand behind it. At last it touched the cool sword. A great, explosive "Ah!" burst from the pale lips, blowing the dust away, as the fingers closed about the hilt.

The touch was like the caress of a lover. From the grip of Gate-Opener came power and returning vigor. As he lay there, his wan cheeks flushed with new health. More even! Whether it was from the prayer or from his desperate desire to go to Ivga's rescue, a strange feeling pulsed through his limbs. In legs that had been numb and lifeless for a year, a prickling sensation grew. It passed and returned again. And when it finally disappeared, he found that his feet would move!

While he marveled, rapt with the wonder of the seeming miracle, he heard voices outside the cottage.

Two men came laughing down the road, talking loudly as they neared the building. Suddenly they became quiet. Careful footsteps came up to the door and paused. A deep hatred came to Dmitri as he lay rigid, listening.

"He has not moved. He is dead," whispered one. "You killed him with that last kick, Wesoskas!"

The other man laughed evilly. "A good deed then. I owed it to him. No man strikes me, but he pays—sometime. He struck me once; did I ever tell you?"

"I believe you did, now that you speak of it," said the smith, sardonically. "Come. The night falls. If any soldier should hear of this and see us here—"

The idiot giggled. "Soon! Soon! I want to talk to him a bit."

Leaning farther through the doorway, he cried, "You in there. Listen to this. She is in town, fastened to the stake. Wouldn't you like to see your imp now?

"She won't kill any more men or blind them for looking at her. We have her fast, and at dawn she burns! The wood is gathered, the pile is ready, and the pitch is at hand. Ha-ha! Old man! Old man! Can you hear me in Hell, old man? Why don't you answer me?"

The smith seized him, horrified at this tormenting of a dead man. "Come, you fool, come away," he urged. "I hear sounds in the wood."

"All right," chuckled the tanner, and then to Helgar: "I've got to leave you, old man. Remember! At dawn she dies. I'm sorry now that I killed you. Really I am. If you could only see it!"

And then his voice was lifted in expostulations against the force his companion was using in dragging him away.

As the complaints became fainter and could no longer be heard, a tenebrous shadow moved with no body to cause it, and squatted, a puddle of blackness, in a corner.

And in the deserted cottage, a thing happened which would have chilled the blood of the idiot tanner.

The form he had thought a corpse raised itself upon its knees. For the first time in a year, Dmitri stood erect upon his feet. For a moment, he listened by the door, then crossed to the wall with steps that were wavery and uncertain. He lifted down the leather harness that would fasten the broadsword to his back and buckled the straps together. Placing Gate-Opener in its sheath, he returned to the door with a surer stride. Though the sword was heavy, he fitted the harness about his shoulders and stood straight in the doorway, looking out over the trees

118

at the stars which gleamed also over Ponkert, a mile away.

Reverently, he bowed his head, believing that his prayer had been answered. Every moment now he felt stronger, although his legs were still weak and trembled beneath Gate-Opener's weight.

Dmitri had never been a religious man. Indeed, one of his frequent sayings was: "If there is a God at all, He must pay more attention to those who are not always bothering Him by asking for something. How weary He must be of begging!" But now it seemed that even the strong were sometimes weak, and with a full heart he would have worshiped and given thanks, but could find no words. And all the while, precious time was fleeting by, never to return.

He raised his hands beseechingly to the stars and cried: "I am coming, Ivga! If you are alive, I will free you or die in Ponkert square. If they have killed you, look down from the parapets of Heaven and watch the wizened souls of Ponkert dead go squealing by to Satan's halls. And Brenryk, watch a Helgar keep a promise!"

He descended the steps and walked slowly into the forest toward the village.

Behind him, a black pool of shadow, darker than the rest of the night shades, flowed down the steps and along the path. It was oddly shaped, as though something stunted and malformed lingered there, suiting its pace to that of the old man just ahead. Yet, there was no one else that could be seen, walking down the path.

At this time, which was about the second hour of the night, a small procession stopped just outside the village. A hiss had sounded from a thicket, and Hugo, returning from a private venture in horse trading to the west of Ponkert, drew rein and half rose in his saddle.

"Who is there?" he said. "Step in front of me!"

"It is you, Hugo?" a cautious whisper came. "I am glad. I have waited hours for you to return."

119

From the bushes hobbled a hunched figure, wrapped about in a long, black cloak. He recognized the wrinkled face as that of the gipsy crone, Clauda, his best friend after Mirko.

"What is it?" he said, startled by her strange look. "What has happened?"

"Don't go through the village, Hugo," she replied, clutching the bridle. "The people will kill you. They have seen you with the Werewolf's daughter, and they will burn you, too!"

"Burn me, too!" His heart almost stopped beating. "Have they burned her?"

"Not yet," was the grim reply. "But in the morning . . ."

"Quick, Mother Clauda! What have they done? Where is she?"

"In the square, bound to the stake on the scaffold. Hugo, what are you going to do?"

The last words were almost a scream, for the boy had leaped from his horse and torn away her cloak.

"I am going to save her," he replied, wrapping the cloak about him and drawing it close about his head.

"They will kill you, Hugo. Is she worth it?" quavered old Clauda, her lips trembling.

He turned to her tenderly and placed his arms about her waist.

"Clauda, you have been a mother to me, and we love each other, do we not? But now my heart lies in Ponkert, and if this girl dies, my life is an empty thing, for she is my worship and we have sworn an oath together. Take the horses to the camp, and if I never return they shall be yours. I have plenty of money with me. Give Mirko a farewell, and this for you."

He bent and kissed the soft, withered lips. They were wet with tears. Then, gently, he disengaged the arms that clung to keep him with her, and he was away.

He ran into the village streets with long strides, making a wide circle to avoid the first row of buildings.

120

Sobbing, Clauda led the horses around the village. With an uncanny prescience, she knew she would never see the boy again. The days ahead would be bleak and dreary without him.

And thus it came about that on the third night of the caravan's stay, from opposite sides of Ponkert came two men, animated with a single purpose. They were pawns in a game that neither could have understood—a game whose beginning was before their known history, and whose end and far reaching events may not yet be done.

C H A P. T E R VIII

Ivga cried out and opened her eyes to a blinding glare. A sputtering torch scorched her face and hair, as the guard bent over her and shook her shoulder roughly.

"What are you talking about?" he snarled. "None of your tricks, vixen! Are you calling me some fiend from hell to serve you, witch? Silence, or I'll slit your tongue! Why don't you answer me? Answer me; to whom were you talking? Why did you say: 'You may!' and 'Yes!' when no one spoke to you. Why, witch?"

With the entering of her body again, Ivga had forgotten the meeting with the master. Now she could only blink into the glare and murmur, "Someone is coming at last," hardly knowing the meaning of the words, for the master had taken back the memory of the meeting as one last mercy.

Still holding her by the shoulder, the guard turned about. His face had turned white with fear, for he was prone to superstition and expected to see some bat-winged creature close by, called from its evil nest by the witch.

A man was standing below at the foot of the steps.

His face was not visible, for a fold of his long, black cloak hid all but his eyes. They glinted like steel in the brilliant moonlight.

The revulsion of feeling was too much for the sentry. "Who are you and what do you want?" he queried boldly. A sepulchral voice issued from the black cloak.

"I am a messenger from Hell for you," it said. "Your place is prepared. Come!"

With slow tread the figure mounted the steps. The sentry backed away as it came higher.

"Stop!" he squeaked in a terrified falsetto. "What do you want?"

The black cloak fell to the ground as the man sprang up the last two steps. The girl gasped "Hugo!" as he flashed her a quick, promising glance, and advanced toward her guard.

"I want the girl and your blood!" he spat. "Death to you, gutter offal!"

The guard, seeing that it was only a man before him, sprang forward roaring. Hugo grinned as a wolf grins. As the guard's sword hissed from its scabbard, the primitive rapier glimmered in the boy's hand like a slender pencil of light. The two blades engaged.

Back across the platform the sentry rushed the lighter man in the first shock of conflict. His longer weapon whirled wickedly and struck sparks as it clashed against the slim, pointed rod that seemed to be always in the way.

Parrying, his fiercest strokes, the rapier slanted from side to side, never thrusting or remaining still, but always retreating before the guard's ferocious slashes. Continually, the saber bit nothing but air, being deftly turned aside in midstroke, before it had reached maximum velocity, and it ever whistled off at a tangent.

They reached the platform's edge, and Hugo, watching his opponent's eyes, read in them a sudden, evil glee, Suspecting something uncertain, therefore to be dreaded, he

123

danced abruptly to the left. As he did so, his groping foot found empty space in place of solid plank. He shot out from the scaffold, falling eight feet to land quite solidly upon the cobblestone pavement of the square.

Almost instantly he was up again, but no longer smiling. Had one watched, he would have noticed that his movements lacked the resilience and spring of a moment before. Three slashes he parried mechanically, dazed by the blow. Then, as his brain cleared, he took the offensive. Enough time had been wasted!

Through tight-clenched teeth, his breath hissed like the angry speech of a snake. The rapier point pressed forward, now menacing, and did not give ground.

All of the guard's experience up to that time had been with cutting weapons—sabers, axes, broadswords, large and ugly tools for hacking, designed to kill or maim with a single blow. Thrusting weapons were likewise clumsy, pikes and spears in a dozen cruel forms and variations; these were the weapons of the time. Small wonder that Ivga had laughed at Hugo's rapier, so small in comparison!

But the guard, hard pressed and fighting for his life against a strange weapon and an unknown method of fighting, would have felt no inclination to jeer, could he have spared the time. A blur was before his eyes, and from his cheek a warm, salty trickle ran into his gasping mouth, where the point of Hugo's weapon had torn in a barely deflected drive for the throat.

"Moonlight is good to die in," menaced the boy. "Are you ready, woman beater?"

This was the first blood drawn during the fight. It had the instant effect of setting the guard wild and reckless so that he rushed into the almost invisible circle of steel.

In fifteen seconds, with three cleverly executed strokes, one side step and a parry, Hugo pinked his antagonist neatly through the fleshy portion of his left shoulder. As the man turned a quarter way around, his arm raised for a blow, the rapier slipped into his right wrist.

With the double power of the upward thrust and the downward blow, the rapier tore through arm and sleeve as it might through paper, leaving the arm useless.

From the guard's nerveless fingers fell the curved sword, slitting the side of Hugo's boot as it clanked upon the stones. This was his only injury in all that strange fight. Quickly reaching with his left hand, the man clutched for the fallen sword. As he lurched forward, the rapier point met him. For an instant, Hugo kept the pose, left hand half behind him, right knee bent, right arm and rapier forming a straight line that ended in the guard's chest.

As a tree falls, so fell the guard, dragging the rapier from Hugo's hand, leaving the boy staring down at him.

Dead! Although he had seen many so, this was his first victory that had ended in death. Suddenly he felt sick in the pit of his stomach. It was so easy to kill a man.

On the scaffold, Ivga spoke wearily. Conquering his squeamishness, Hugo tugged at his blade. The flesh clung about it as though loth to let it go. Before it was free, he was forced to pull at it with all his strength.

With a swift stroke, he wiped clean the rapier upon the dead man's coat. Holding the slender rod in one hand, he drew his dagger with the other, and leaped up the steps of the scaffold. The dagger made short work of the leather thongs that bound her body to the pillar. With the guard's keys, he released her from the chains.

She opened her eyes and smiled at him. It was a pale, wan smile that wrung his heart, as he released her from her cruel bonds.

"I knew you would come," she whispered, and her arms went out to him.

As she took a step forward, her limbs gave way beneath her. Paralyzed by the tightness of the straps, she fell to her knees upon the rough planks. Instantly he was holding her close. Her voice sobbed thickly to him, muffled, for her face was pressed hard against his cheek.

"Oh, Hugo! I cannot walk! What are we to do?"

In that moment, feeling her dependence upon him and her implicit trust that somehow he would save her, the boy became a man. A deep love and yearning to protect welled up within him, called by her helplessness, and he replied:

"We will go at once to the camp. Mirko will hide us. Come!" And he stood up.

The girl attempted to rise, but the pain was too great and she collapsed again. Her wrists were deeply cut by the chains, and, as she chafed her ankles, she could feel no sensation in her hands.

"You go," she said finally. "Leave me here. I shall only be a burden to you. The watchman will come through here soon, and we cannot both escape. Flee, Hugo, before the alarm is given, or we both shall die! And I don't want you to die, too!"

He grinned. "You rave. Did you really believe I would go away from you now? No, if we are killed, we die together. Let us go to Mirko."

He sheathed his weapons, lifted her in his arms, and descended the steps.

"Get the book on the beam, Hugo," said Ivga. "It is mine."

And, with the book in her arms, Hugo carried her proudly across the deserted square, eery in the white moonglare, and peopled now only by the few stray dogs that skulked in the shadows. They were lean curs that kept an odd silence and followed close behind.

They entered a narrow street and left the square some distance behind before either spoke.

Ivga lay quietly in his arms, watching his stern face for some sign of weakness. Although his lips were tightly compressed, his breath came even and unhurried as he swung along, covering ground rapidly with long strides.

"Am I heavy, Hugo?" she asked once. "Set me down a little and rest."

His answer was to crush her tighter against his chest.

"You are not heavy at all, little Ivga. I could carry you forever!"

She clasped her arms around his neck, relieving him of a little of the strain, the book in her lap, and kissed him with a swift movement. After that, her brown hair sank down upon his shoulder and the tired eyes closed.

Tenderly he bore her, for her cuts and bruises were many. He thought she slept.

They entered an alley which opened off the side street, giving a view of dark tree tops against the stars. His aim was to reach the gipsy encampment, if possible, and to place himself and the girl under the protection of the chief. He felt certain that the cowardly villagers would not dare to attack a strong force.

Finally, he was compelled to release his burden and rest. While he rubbed his cramped arms, he saw from the tail of his eye a stealthy movement behind the corner of a building. It was as though someone had peered out and darted back.

Sword in hand, he ran back. Nothing was in sight, and he returned to the girl. Again he gathered her carefully into his arms and strode off, now often turning to look behind. There was no stir or movement.

They had continued for a couple of minutes, and his suspicions were almost lulled, when Ivga's head lifted from his shoulder. Her curls brushed his cheek.

"Someone is following us," she whispered, her lips tickling his ear.

Without answering, he quickened his pace.

A large building was before them. Once around the corner he laid her down, made his sword ready, and waited.

A head poked cautiously around the corner. It saw the waiting blade, jaw dropping in horror and surprise, and was instantly withdrawn. It was the watchman!

Hugo leaped in pursuit of the fleeing man, who yelled with every bound, imagining the point was already in his back.

The race was short. Hugo rapidly overtook the pursued. There was a brief flash of steel, rapier against dagger, and the cries stopped. But the mischief had been done.

Windows began to creak open, and voices to shout from house to house, as he ran back to Ivga, hugging the shadows.

"Quick!" he panted. "To the gipsies. They will help us!" And he stooped to pick her up.

"No," she exclaimed. "it is too far. They could catch us long before we could get there. We will go to the river, find a boat, and drift downstream until we are far away."

"But we will have to go back through the village to reach the boats," he protested.

"Come!" She tugged impatiently at him. "I know a way. If we climb that mountain and go down the other side, the river is just below us. Dmitri—" she choked on the word—"and I had a little boat that we hid in the rocks. We used it to sail on the river and fish from."

"Can we go around the mountain?" he gasped, doubting her strength for such a climb.

"No," she replied jerkily. "Thick brush on one side. The river is too deep on the other. Can't swim. I can climb. Hurry!"

CHAPTER IX

A man bearing a mighty sword had reached the corpse of the watchman. At his back skulked a double shadow—his own and a second beside it; yet only one man was visible in the moonlight.

The man bent over the body and nodded admiringly as he saw the hole. It has been placed, skillfully, beneath the third rib. He passed on upon weak and tottering limbs, chuckling to himself. It had been a neat death, and he recognized that the cause of it had been the same weapon that laid low the sentry by the scaffold.

He had more than a suspicion that he knew who bore the weapon, whose like had never been seen before in Ponkert. He knew, also, who had cut the bonds of that prisoner the sentry had guarded in the village square.

The man hobbled around the corner of the building. A long way off he saw two people running across the fields toward the mountain. He shouted, but they were too far away to hear. Using Gate-Opener as a crutch, he followed.

Beside him, if he had turned his head, he might have seen two shadows slip over the ground.

In the village, lights were beginning to show in houses and torches to wave in the streets. The crowd gathered, all confusion and shouting, about the scaffold in the square. They scurried madly about in search of the fugitives, each one looking carefully where he thought the werewolf would least likely to be. There was much crowding together.

"Safety in numbers! The Werewolf's daughter is loose! They went that way!" And off they would pour in another direction, howling like madmen.

Soon, there was a great deal of deserting from the ranks, as the most lukewarm and half-hearted members decided that the night was too chill for delicate lungs, and it would be as well to wait for morning.

Consequently, it was twenty minutes before the body of the watchman was discovered, sprawled in a dark alley, and the two who fled had climbed the mountain.

Dmitri had just reached its base when lights began to wink and flare across the fields. These lights were not needed for illumination on the moonlit paths, but were brought because it was well known that a werewolf feared artificial light.

The road over the mountain was not a fair or level causeway, but a steep declivity. It was crusted with rock and round pebbles until the very top where it was notched and grooved, pinnacles on either hand, forty feet or more of black rock clothed in summer by dainty flowers that no hand would ever pluck or nostrils smell.

At the bottom of this tremendous groove, two figures lay panting after the tedious struggle up the shifting slope. Stones still clattered down, knocking dryly together in rush and chattering hurry. The excited babble of their going droned up to the two in a murmur of sound, and though the rolling pebbles gathered others with them, becoming a tiny landslide as they poured into the valley, the roar of their final plunge came up to the twin peaks as a faint and airy whisper. So remote were they, in their awful majesty, from the passions of men.

The boy and girl rested. They had climbed the slope and had arrived at steps cut in the solid rock. These steps were carved by hands that were long since dust, to the purpose of making a watch tower for the castle that lay in ruins, far away.

Up the steps and along a dangerous path hanging over a straight drop of a hundred feet they had passed. At its finish there were more steps around a boulder, and then a steep climb over the lip of the cliff, directly above a giddy drop. One false step meant death.

"I can see now why this is a short cut," panted the boy. "This place was made for goats and children."

A sudden noise from far below, a new tinkling of stones set in motion, startled them.

"Oh! They have found us!" cried the girl. "They are coming to kill us. Oh, Hugo, save me. I love you!"

He held her tightly until trust and confidence in his protection and strength reassured her. Finally, he loosened his grip and sprang to the edge of the cliff. Far beneath a black, indistinct figure moved up the treacherous gravel slope. It was a figure that climbed slowly and stopped often, as though the road was most difficult. As he watched, it progressed higher and nearer.

A long way behind, the fields gleamed and twinkled with many flecks of dancing light which drifted toward the mountain like fireflies in interweaving love dance over a marsh. Still more distant, Ponkert was ablaze with lights. Hugo heard a thin, faded murmur like distant rapids far off, where in mad hubbub and howling rout the people surged about an immense bonfire in the square.

Hugo swore softly to himself and moved back upon the cliff. With both hands, he was struggling with a loose rock to roll down upon the climber, when the girl, who had also looked over the edge, prevented his design.

"Quick," she whispered, fearfully. "Let us go to the boat. He is still far away. When he reaches here we will be gone, and he will have no idea where we went."

Her logic was indisputable, for a falling stone would have betrayed their presence on the mountain, even if this man were killed.

Hugo reluctantly allowed himself to be drawn along the cleft in the mountain without another downward glance. Had either looked again, they could hardly have failed by this time to recognize the massive sword which swung many times when the climber staggered on the dangerous path. Along its five foot length, it flamed in the moonlight like the demon-forged sword of Ibn Asad Iraf, which the genii formed of the white ash of thunderbolts.

He had passed the gravel slide and was half up the mountain when Hugo and the girl commenced the descent of the other side. Here, too, the path was narrow and steep, if less precipitous. But the danger was equal, for there was no moon to light this side.

Down slippery steps they stumbled; along crumbling, rotten ledges drowned in shadows. They crashed through bushes and felt their way about in the dark, all the while tottering precariously on the edge of destruction.

From below it seemed that the river came up to meet them all too slowly. At length, the girl could see the little boat rocking by its secret wharf hidden in the reeds. The dampness and chill of the river fog was rising about them when the mob commenced to climb the gravel slide.

High above them on the path below the cliff rim, Dmitri rested, leaning upon the sword, Gate-Opener.

The struggle had been hard and long for his feeble limbs, and only the deathly fear of being too late to help his loved one had kept him moving. Burdened by the heavy sword, it seemed a miracle to him that the climb had been accomplished. But the worst was over. Only a few steps separated him now from the girl he worshipped. And, knowing that once upon the mountain, the three could hold off an army, he rejoiced.

The torches below mounted higher, relentlessly nearer. The shouts of their bearers became clear.

Wearily, Dmitri walked toward the steps that led up to the cleft above, almost overbalanced by the great broadsword.

"Ivga!" he called, when he topped the cliff's edge. When there was no answer, he forgot caution and cried loudly: "Ivga, Hugo! Where are you! It is Dmitri!"

There was no sound but the whistle of the wind through the mountain top ravine and the dry whisper of pebbles rattling below, set in motion by many feet.

Then, gripping his heart with a chill of foreboding, came the memory of the boat upon the river. He began to run along the bottom of the little gorge. Perhaps he was too late.

And looking over the edge of the opposite cliff, he saw them, half lost in the fog that streamed about them and nearly to the river.

Realization came that he could not reach them in time to save himself. Should they learn of his presence, he knew that they would return to rescue him or die in the process. Consequently, he forbore to speak and watched silently as they dropped lower in the fog, save once, when he whispered with lips that trembled, "Goodbye, little daughter, goodbye."

For a long time he lay watching them as they clambered down the cliff, until his eyes blurred so that he could see them no longer. Angrily he dashed away the tears, denying even to himself that he was sad.

"I am not sad!" he cried to the stars. "I am happy, Brenryk, happy! Can you hear? Wherever they may go, whatever they may do, it will be I that has made it possible. I promised you, oh tragic soul, that I would guard her with my life. Watch me if you can and see how a Helgar keeps an oath. With my blood I buy her happiness. And she will be happy because of me. I will be happy because she will never know I died to save her. Oh, Brenryk, I am glad, glad that I am here tonight! Not everyone can die for the one he loves best in all the world!"

Trailing the immense sword behind him, he ran back. In the center of the pass, he chose his position with care, selecting a spot where the two sides of the notch came closest, like the narrow point of the letter M. And of the M, each angle was a pinnacle of rock forty feet in height.

There was only one spectator. The shadow that had accompanied Dmitri thus far disengaged itself from his shadow. It rose like a wisp of fog along the cliff until it reached the top of the left hand pinnacle, where it stopped and became one with the other shadows on the wall. Two spots of light glistened where it paused, like moonlight reflected from moist, shiny eyeballs.

In his chosen spot, Dmitri made ready. The floor was not level except where he stood, and sloped in a gentle descent in the direction of the river—more steeply toward the other cliff. It was strewn with rocks that had fallen from the twin pinnacles.

These Dmitri cleared from his platform, casting them in the path up which attackers would soon climb. He could hear them toiling up the loose gravel as he dislodged the last moving stone and rolled it down. The cursing and the rattling of stones was very near.

A lurid, smoky glare rose over the edge of the cliff. A heavy thump, followed by a chorus of jeers and coarse laughter. He ran back to the center of the pass and waited in a niche in the wall.

The murky smoke and glare of the torches shining on the rock were like the sun rising over the lip of the ledge. Then three bright flames burst into sight together. The old man crouched closer in his niche, where the light would not find him, whispering to his sword, "Soon! Soon! Dost thou hunger? Patience, but a little longer!"

While he patted Gate-Opener's hilt and crooned to it,

the people were gathering on the ledge.

Up they came, breathing hard and sweating from the climb, looking about with curiosity. Although the mountain was near home, many had never climbed since they were children, and the surroundings were strange.

Well contented to rest, those foremost waited until all had come before essaying the next climb. When the troop was gathered, Dmitri saw that they numbered perhaps a rough two score persons. He chuckled to himself, stroking the smooth blade.

"Only forty, Gate-Opener, only forty! How many will there be after they have played with you, sweet chum?"

The mass began to move. One hundred feet away, seventy feet, forty-five . . . Dmitri cast one last look around him, saw that only three could approach him at once in the narrow passage, and took a deep breath. They were thirty feet away when he sprang into the open, his back against a large boulder immovably imbedded in the rock.

None saw his leap. One second he was not; the next, there he stood leaning on the great sword, square in the center of the path as though he had sprung from the living rock. Then, with the design of halting the mob, he opened his lips. From them pealed forth a strident inhuman screech sounding like nothing else in either Heaven or Earth. It was the gutteral Hi-yi-yi of the Cossack about to join in battle!

Cries of fear arose from the crowd as they saw the apparition and stopped. Above them, upon his pinnacle, the master chuckled and settled himself for the show.

The curtain had risen, the players were at hand, the first line had been spoken—the play was about to begin!

The master promised himself a rare entertainment. He had tested the mettle of Ponkert men before, and he was well assured that they would not pass until the boy and girl were far down the river. So he hoped, for the girl's escape meant much to him.

The report that the maniac's kick had been fatal to Dmitri had been circulated in the village and believed, for it was well known that the cripple had not left his chair for many days. So now they looked at this specter arisen from the dead, and the superstitious mob surged back in horror. Faces blanched, while pale lips muttered half forgotten charms for the laying of the restless dead who will not sleep o' nights, and twitching fingers crossed hearts with hurried strokes.

And Dmitri moved! The thirsty sword swept through thinly complaining air in dazzling circular swoop.

"Come!" he howled, as he swung the sword, the red glare of the torches running along the blade like dripping blood. "Come and kiss Death."

And a man moved—the idiot tanner, spurred forward by hate. Braver by reason of this hate, he came forward on trembling limbs, with outstretched hand and ingratiating smile. Deceitful and placatory words waited to be uttered in case the thing was a phantom, but behind his back the other hand closed upon the heavy dagger to be used if it was only a man that blocked the way.

Dmitri leaned upon his sword and waited.

Nearer the tanner came to the specter, and nearer still. His hoarse, frightened breathing was all that could be heard—that and oars a-thump on the river.

Fingers seeking, touched and found solid flesh beneath material cloth, and with a cry, the madman darted out his dagger in swift and cowardly thrust.

Slashing down as the falcon swoops for prey screamed the thirsty sword. It shore through the profaning arm—and the hand, still clasped about the dagger's hilt, spun into the shadows. Then, with a quick reverse stroke, the old man struck again, so that ten feet of air was the only union between the tanner's head and the shoulders that had born it.

While the body stood upon limply crumpling legs, the

imprisoned air within its lungs rushed forth so that the dead man seemed to speak in coughing, liquid grunts. The head rolled, jaw agape in stupid amaze, and stood upon its stub, as though it watched the battle through fast glazing eyes.

For a moment the crowd stood, shocked. Then it surged forward, axes and knives waving high among the wild and frantic torches.

On the river, the pursued found the boat fast to the wharf. The river had fallen so low that the shallow water would not float it over the muddy bottom with the weight of the two in it.

Hugo was forced to jump over the side and push mightily through the reeds, sinking deep into the mud. After some moments of agonized struggle, he felt harder ground beneath his feet. The keel of the boat grated on gravel and finally floated free. It swung sluggishly in the still water near the shore while he climbed in and took the oars.

A confused murmur of voices drifted down from above, and the girl turned to listen.

"They have reached the top, Hugo!" she exclaimed.

The oars dug deep and the boat shot forward with the sudden pounce of a cat. The stout oars creaked and bent with the stroke. Hugo clung to the shore beneath the overhanging cliff in dread of falling stones which he knew would follow, should they be seen.

The skin along his spine crawled, and his scalp prickled with the momentary anticipation of the shouts that would mean they were discovered. He thought of the rumble of falling boulders that would follow the shouts. Even the splash of one dropping from that height would be sufficient to fill the boat, leaving them helpless in the water and exposed to their pursuers.

Ivga, mercifully ignorant of their peril, was listening for further sounds.

Five more strokes would take them to safety. Three had been taken when suddenly a wild, unearthly screech pealed out from above. The boat was exactly below the notch in the mountain top.

It was Dmitri's wordless yell as he stepped from concealment to face the mob. Something in the tone struck home to Ivga, but believing Dmitri dead, she did not associate the voice with his. Still it was familiar, and her puzzled brows knit together in vague, indefinable worry. It seemed to her as though she should know who or what screamed.

Strange was the voice, and yet somehow—not strange!

She put up her hand to attract Hugo's attention. "Stop!" she commanded in a low voice. "Did you hear that noise? What could it have been?"

Hugo had heard the screech in spite of his exertions, and recognized it for what it was—the voice of a man. But he read into it a dreadful meaning and suspected that they were seen. Consequently, he had no thought of hesitating there in that most dangerous spot.

Not wishing to alarm the girl, he answered carelessly, "'Twas nothing. A night bird crying, perhaps," and with another fierce stroke, the boat shot into midstream. The rushing current caught them, and the two were swept away.

Still, Ivga was vaguely disturbed. She listened long, ready to trap any vagrant sound, but none came. As they were carried away from the mountain, and the lights of Ponkert became more remote, the possibility of hearing the uproar that was soon to take place in the notch disappeared.

At last Ivga sank down into the bottom of the boat and lay there while Hugo rowed sturdily. Seeing him there, she was reassured and placed her head in the hollow of her arm to try to sleep.

Dmitri's back was firm against the boulder, and his left side was partly protected by an outcrop of rock as the man

138

pack closed in upon him. As a result, he was not entirely exposed to the villagers' weapons which began to lick in and out like frozen tongues of flame.

Those who had swords, feeling their superiority over the common herd who were armed by more menial weapons, had taken the front of battle.

Dung forks were present; flails, clubs and pikes; spears and staves of wood waved in the torch smoke like limbs of a leafless forest. The humble spade was conspicuous; axe and hatchet glittered; and the knives reached out like an old witch's one long fang.

It was a motley crew, and motley was the arming of it. But at the fore, swords were slithering and blades hissed —as though in the darkness Death sat, whetting his scythe.

And the harvest was not long in the reaping, for the time that Dmitri had spent polishing his well beloved Gate-Opener, over and over until it had attained an unbelievable edge, had not been wasted. With a heap of bodies like a windrow in the haying field, a bloody barrier began to rise across the narrow way.

The blades kissed. Rusty weapons that had long hung in disuse upon the walls of some peasant's hut were wielded by unskillful hands. They were heavy, ancient tools for murder. They circled in clumsy stroke and parry, stroke again—and parry, third stroke, no parry—and so fell; clean, unblooded, unfleshed, racing their owners to the ground. And other blades took their turn.

The path grew slippery, a tiny rivulet trickling black in the torchlight. It came from gaping throat, from riven chest, from shattered skull, while panting, reckless men struggled up the steep.

They slipped in the red ooze, slid and fell on the loose rocks, and stumbled over the bodies of those that had gone on before. On they came, drunk with the reek of blood —to stagger back wailing for a space through bubbling throats. Through eyes that were slit and never would see

139

again, they searched for one more glimpse, or felt their way with stumps of arms through the eager throng.

Many remained to add their bodies to the rampart of flesh, but a pitiful debris of battle crawled back, every step a separate agony.

Dmitri's sword was sharp!

Several died not knowing the blow that slew them, slashed into eternity by a cold edge like a breath of wind upon their throats. While their blades shone unsullied by any stain save rust, Gate-Opener, as it rose and fell, drank deep, bit hard, and lusted for the next, swooping hither and thither in hungry search for prey.

Men began to cry out that it was no man that opposed them, but a devil. They cried, too, that the sword lived.

And Dmitri held the narrow way!

A lull came in the fighting while men moved the wounded from their path, and Dmitri tugged the bodies of the dead into a heap before him.

The villagers were clustering together for a rush, when a voice roared out in that place of death, as though a fiend was merry. It was a hideous, ghastly laugh! Again it howled out, and then wild and exultant:

> Shen, shen, shivagen.
>   Swing the steel, swing again.
> Ride, ride to our play.
>   Slay! slay!

Dmitri made mock of his enemies in a song of the steppe.

Then they were at him again, three together, scrambling doggedly over the heap of bodies, one with a pike and two with clubs.

Gate-Opener swung up, and the pike rattled in two pieces on the rock, its holder impaled himself upon the sword. Swift disengagment, for, cursing, the others were upon him. A flurry of clubs, dull thuds, a sharp cry, and

140

one was reeling back, his left arm severed at the shoulder. Stupidly he moved; as one who sees the calamity which has befallen, yet cannot believe. The other man lay prone, another body for the barricade.

Those of the mob that were left wavered. They drew back, milled together, and tried to renew their courage. While Dmitri was exhausted, he did not allow himself a moment's rest. He was busy fixing the fallen swords and pikes in the barricade so that the points projected outward to present a thorny hedge of steel points, behind which he waited.

The boat had traveled a half mile down the stream, propelled by Hugo's strong muscles and the current. Despite her exhaustion, Ivga was unable to rest.

She was leaving her home with a stranger, bound for a new land. And, while her life in the village had been a thing of horror to be best forgotten, it was still her home. It was the only home she had ever known.

Dmitri was dead, murdered in his cabin, without being able to lift a finger toward his defense or hers. Trapped like a rabbit in its burrow, he had died. And all that she held dear had died with him, the only father she had ever known. What could become of her now?

Hugo's face looked hard in the moonlight, set and stern, lips compressing with each stroke of the oars. Carrying her away! Where? And to what fate? Perhaps his father, the lord, would not like a girl that brought only the clothes she stood in. Perhaps Hugo would not love her long; man's fancy was fickle, so Dmitri had told her, and if he should leave her, what was there to do, but die?

These and other thoughts flitted through her mind while she lay there intently staring at him. At last he became conscious of her fearful gaze and looked down, smiling.

How his face changed when he smiled. Little crinkles about the eyes appeared that one would never suspect existed. Suddenly she was positive that he loved her.

141

"Are you tired, Ivga?" he asked, ever so softly, placing his hand on her forehead.

The gentle touch soothed her wild fancies. She nodded with both eyes closed, and clasped his hand in both her own. The little hands were hot and fevered, but reassurance and peace flowed into her from Hugo's cool, hard palm. Quietly, she relaxed and slipped into a sleep of exhaustion.

Upon the mountain, a young man was pleading with the mob. It was the brother of the slain woodchopper whose body had been found in the forest. He gesticulated and stamped about the end of the small ravine, and a fanatical light shone in his eyes.

"Come!" he raved at them. "Are you men or sheep? We are forty and he is one! Even rats fight when they are in packs. You are worse than rats!"

There was a deathlike silence of some seconds, broken only by the groans of a faceless man dragging himself down the slope.

Suddenly a voice spoke somewhere within the crowd, with a certain pleased surprise, like one who has just discovered a new and amusing fact. Two words only. "Were forty!"

"Who said that?" cried the fanatic, glaring angrily about. There was no reply.

The broken man lurched on, crawling like some eyeless slug toward the clifff edge and the people. They shrank away from him as though he were a leper.

An uncanny feeling was fast becoming a conviction, that any who had felt the bite of that long sword was accursed!

From the sides they shrank away, and from in front, until he struggled through a lane of silent watchers and reached the edge of the cliff. He stopped, sensing vacancy before him, the shattered head swaying blindly to and fro. No one moved to save him. A hoarse, puzzled croak bubbled from his red mask of a face. He heaved forward on his arms, balanced on the edge, toppled and fell.

Men breathed again, the strain broken. Shamefacedly, they dodged one another's eyes, each thinking, "Why didn't I stop him before he fell? Why am I such a coward?"

The young man seized the presented opportunity.

"He did that!" he shouted, pointing at Dmitri, a dim figure in the past. "Now! Once more! The werewolf cowers beyond him! Shall we wait longer?"

With deep growls of rage and shame they answered him, and the mass surged forward in the last charge. It was a ponderous, irresistable wave of bodies that rolled on to the attack. They reached the barricade, and there were shrieks from those in front who were pinned upon the spikes that projected from it. But there was no turning back.

Over the bodies of their writhing comrades climbed the mob, pressing on to present a front of spears and pikes.

In vain Dmitri struck and struck again. The foe was too great. Feeling his strength ebbing fast, the old man knew that his hour was upon him.

Back he was crowded, as they mounted over the still living bodies that were spiked on the barrier of projecting swords.

As he fought, Dmitri recollected the words of the old gipsy, and realized that this was the scene she had described in her vision.

A red mass of gashes, he staggered back still farther, Gate-Opener swinging like a monstrous sickle in the hands of Death, no longer bright and shining, its edge nicked and dulled on the bones of men.

A momentary lull in the fighting. The way was clogged with dead, and as they cleared the path, Dmitri, howling an unintelligible battle yell, went beserk.

In his turn, he charged—his last wild strokes a mad effort to keep them back from the river ten seconds more—for within his body something had broken, and he knew

143

the end was near.

Gate-Opener whistled down and a man collapsed like a slashed sack of meal—eviscerated, his life juices flowing from him. Then, while Dmitri still hacked his road through flesh, his right foot came upon something that rolled and threw him down.

Instantly he was up, but too late. Three spears took him, and he fell. With his last failing remnants of sight, he saw that he had stepped upon the tanner's head, and that Gate-Opener lay close by, shattered beyond mending. Both were leaving together—the man and the sword.

He smiled wryly again. "A dead man shall slay thee!" he quoted the gipsy woman, and his eyes closed.

Over his body, cursing, pushing, the remainder of the villagers rushed on to the river. But they were too late, for the two were far beyond.

Behind them, Dmitri raised himself upon an elbow, gasping faintly with his last breath. "Brenryk! Have I not kept my word to you?" and so died.

Far down the river, the little boat raced south, rocking in the rushing current. The youth who guided it began to sing softly, far from earshot of the village of Ponkert.

As the song was finished, and the voice, mellow and young, died away in the distance, the soul of Dmitri Helgar passed from its war torn body. It drove past the master perched upon his rock and began the journey to the place where such souls go.

And the master, as he sped upon his way, gave Dmitri that sign of approbation which is given from one valiant spirit to another; for, had he not served the master well?

Of the red wrath and ruin that raged in Ponkert that day, when the soldiers of the Black Brigade learned of the glorious fight and sought out those that were left from the battle, taking a strong revenge for their captain, it is not necessary to speak.

Carried along on the bosom of the river, the little boat went rocking downstream, while above the sky reddened with morning.

In the stern, Hugo trailed an oar for a rudder, no longer rowing and more than half asleep. He nodded over his task, but was not so far gone that he did not know when the girl's little fingers slipped into his hand lying limp on the seat.

He opened one eye enough to see that hers were closed, and that she slept. Apparently, she was dreaming, for her lips were curved in the loveliest smile he had ever seen upon her face. She looked much like a little child, lying there asleep, her thick curls in pretty disarray.

Carefully, that he might not wake her, he disengaged her fingers from his hand, removed his coat and spread it over her. Then, one calloused palm held the oar again, and the other stroked a curl that lay conveniently near.

At the light touch, she smiled once more, as though her dreams were pleasant. Dimly, happily, she knew that she would never be lonely any more.

CHAPTER X

So we see them, two wanderers in Arcadia, almost hidden from us now by the intervening years, dropping down the river, each finding joy in the other, perfect mates.

It would be too long a story to relate the whole of that journey—how from this river they entered another whose name we do not know, but might have been the Drave, the Save, or the Theiss, and were carried on. How they went ashore by night and procured food in many manners, sometimes a vegetable garden suffering from their visits, sometimes a hen roost or dairy. For, although Hugo had money, it must be saved for ship passage when they reached the sea.

And they had far indeed to go. There were seven or eight hundred miles of travel upon the Danube alone. They were miles full of natural perils, more dangerous even than the men they encountered—and they were many.

A separate tale could be made of their adventures on the river—how they passed by cities in the night unhindered, by castles that frowned down at them, two midgets in a cockle shell, but accosted them not for toll; how river pirates, less lenient, twice attacked them, sweeping out in long, low skiffs from the hidden coves in the river bank.

That fight at least deserves a chapter—how they howled out their cry of "Blood and death!" as the skiff came near, and evil faces leered at the two in the boat; how the knitting needle knitted well, unraveling soul from body; and how another fought beside the girl and boy so that the attackers dotted the sullen water, and the fishes fed for days. For, invisible to them, a thing brooded over the boat, a creature powerful to aid and protect, and, unknowing they were owned by it, they unconsciously did its bidding. To their enemies it was a horror by night and a terror by day. Men's brains were so mazed that sword strokes and spear thrusts missed their marks.

The master was leaving Ponkert and Hungary for a new hunting ground, and woe to any who would hinder his journey or harm those who traveled under his protection.

Among the perils, those of the river must be mentioned.

Once they passed the Kazan Defile and the terrible Iron Gates, the rest was less hazardous, but all the way was from one danger into another. And they did not dare to travel by land. So along the stream from old Moldova to Orsova and the Iron Gates they floated, where the river is enclosed by mountains and rocky banks, and even landing was difficult at that time.

Through the rocks, sand banks and whirlpools they went, sometimes wet all day long from the spray. Often they were sick and weary, but ever they pressed on, each night one day's journey nearer the sea.

Once their boat was sunk in the terrible Stenka Rapids, a bank of rocks extending almost across the river, most of them visible when the water was low, and eleven hundred yards long. Below these, they stole another boat and went on.

Through the vast swamp of the Danube delta, they reached the coast of the Black Sea from the Sulina mouth of the river. Here, when the sea rose even a few inches, the banks of the river could be known only by clusters of wretched hovels built on piles and narrow strips of sand. It was a wild, open seaboard, strewn with wrecks—the only guide for mariners to locate the position of the shallows.

The people were half starved, inbred, atavistic creatures, wreckers by nature, and hardly human. Here, the two were afraid and did not linger.

Where now is a first class port with a town of several thousand, lighthouses and floating elevators, it was only by chance that they obtained passage by ship. At Constantinople they shipped again for the last time. Most of their money was gone, and it was more for pity than for gain that a captain agreed to carry the wanderers to France.

And so, they reached the sea and ships, and from the sea they came at last to Blois.

TO THE READER

If you enjoyed this book, you will be glad to know that there are many others just as well written, just as interesting, to be had in the Fiction House Press Library.

You will find the Fiction House Press Library online at

www.FictionHousePress.com